I0670880

LOVE SWEAT TEARS

The Thomas Satherwaite Saga.

A Novel by Colin Setterfield.

Based on a true story.

TABLE OF CONTENTS

11. Ambition is a good servant but a bad master. – unknown.

12. The honey is sweet but the bee has a sting. – Ben Franklin.

13. Marriage is more than finding the right person. It's being the right person. –unknown.

14. The only real mistake is the one from which we learn nothing. –J. Powell.

15. There's no love without pain. –Irving Stone.

16. It is solitary drinking that makes drunkards. –Nathaniel West.

17. Drinking makes such fools of people, and people are such fools to begin with... –Robert Benchley.

18. A bend in the road is not the end of the road, unless you fail to make the turn.—Unknown.

19. Once you choose hope, anything is posible. –Christopher Reeve.

20. The real voyage of discovery consists not in seeking new landscapes but in having new eyes. –Marcel Proust.

21. It takes two flints to make a fire. –L.M. Alcott.

22. Out of the frying pan, into the fire. –John Heywood.

23. The supreme irony of life is that hardly anyone gets out alive—R.A Heinlein.

24. Time is limited and some opportunities never repeat themselves. —Belle de Jour.

25. If you are not living on the edge you are taking up too much room. —Jayne Howard.

26. Nothing succeeds like success. —unknown.

27. To accept defeat is nine-tenths of defeat itself. —Francis Crawford.

28. Don't run from your weakness, you will only give it   strength.—Stephen Richards.

29. The greatest pain that comes from love, is loving someone you can never have. —un known.

30. Parents wonder why the streams are bitter when they themselves have poisoned the fountain. —John Locke.

31. Drink moderately for drunkenness neither keeps a secret nor observes a promise. —Miguel de Cervantes Saavedra.

32. Tis better to have loved and lost than never to have loved at all. —Tennyson.

33. If there were no bad people, there would be no good lawyers. —Charles Dickens.

34. The way to love anything is to realize that it might be lost. —G.K Chesterton.

35. Law is order and good law is good order. —Aristotle

36. The law helps those who watch, not those who sleep. —Proverb.

37. I am not afraid of death, I just don't want to be   there when it happens. —Woody Allen.

38. Love will find a way. —unknown.

39. Conclusion

Introduction

My brother once said to me, Thomas—be careful what you wish for—success comes at a price. In retrospect he's philosophy turned out to be correct. When I think back on it now I have often wondered if my present success validates the loss and sacrifice it incurred.

Willy-John and I fought in the second Anglo Boer War on the side of the British Kingdom against the South African Boers, a group of white, dissident farmers, who sought independence. The Boers, descendant from a seventeenth-century Dutch colony first formed in the Cape, and spread North, toward the Limpopo River.

In November of 1899 we joined up with Lord Methuen's force for the Battle of the Modder River, a most famous skirmish, which found us trapped on open ground and almost cut to pieces by the Boers—we lost many comrades on the day of the conflict.

One month before the end of the war in 1902, on a day my brother and I thought death might overtake us our detail ran into a party of Boer marauders from the Free State region, with numbers much greater than ours. It happened at a creek in the Western Cape farming area. With little cover and no time to retrieve our horses, Willy-John and

I fled through the stream on foot but a Boer bullet tore through my brother's leg and brought him down. I came to his assistance and the two of us hobbled along in an attempt to catch up with our party. The sudden flight took us toward the foothills where we stopped to take a quick rest amongst a few fynbos trees. Desperate for a place to hide I helped Will climb onto the lower branches of a large tree and we hid amongst its leaves.

Hours later the enemy moved off to another area and we escaped through a field toward a farmhouse situated at the foot of a kopje.

On arrival at the Boer abode we hid in a rustic, old barn filled with oxen yokes, broken wagon wheels and farm implements—I judged the time to be after five-thirty in the evening. We bedded down on some cut grass to wait out the night. A quick look at my brother's leg revealed the need for medical attention—I knew it would be much worse by the time morning came.

This's when our fortunes took a peculiar turn.

∞∞

ONE

Good things come when you least expect them. —*unknown*

"Who is in there?" The deep voice of a man called out to us in the Afrikaans language. I raised my Lee Metford ready to shoot in anticipation of a confrontation but Willy-John, always the more level-headed, placed his hand on the muzzle and pushed it down. I could sense the pain reflected in his voice as he gave an answer.

"Sir, we were chased by a party of Boers and became separated from our detail. We are members of the British army and mean you no harm. I have been wounded and request some help."

A few seconds silence followed Will's words. Then a woman spoke.

"If you promise no harm I will take a look at your injury."

She displayed the typical, heavy Afrikaans accent natural to the Boer Nation. The Afrikaners, so called because of their language—Afrikaans, evolved from the initial Caucasian, Dutch colony at the Cape, to form the greater community of white South Africans, before the arrival of the British.

I stood to help Willy-J to his feet and together we hobbled out toward them. The man and his wife took a step back to allow us an easy exit through the single door of the barn. Behind them a younger woman stood with an oil lantern.

The farmer's wife led us to the kitchen door of the farmhouse, an old pastoral abode with a thatched roof, held up by rough timber beams. The compact kitchen sported a coal-fired stove and the cozy heat warmed our weary bones. I deposited Will on one of two chairs adjacent to a wooden table and tore away his trouser-leg to expose the damage.

"This is a nasty wound," said the young woman, whom I judged to be about twenty years old. "We need to remove the bullet before you get an infection."

I looked at Willy-J with concern but he seemed un-phased by the prospect. He gazed into the young woman's eyes and said, "Do what you need to do—you can do anything to me you want."

The girl blushed slightly and displayed a mock irritation at the comment but I could see my brother's words made her feel good. Her pleasant features and curvaceous, strong body typified those of a farmer's daughter. I could not find myself drawn to her, however as she represented the enemy, a consideration my brother chose to ignore.

I must acknowledge, Willy-J had a way with women. He always managed to win them over—made them feel safe with him. I did not possess the same talent. As the younger brother I felt at a disadvantage. Will's experience and charisma far out-weighed my own. I hate to confess it but he provided the brains behind all our decisions.

He convinced my mother to continue with the boarding-house after my father's death and showed her how to run it in a more productive fashion—all his idea. My brick-layers apprentice-ship and my first job—his suggestion. Willy-J's advice always led to our successes but I never allowed myself to become a prisoner of his shadow.

I saw the way he looked at this girl; an angel sent from heaven for his personal benefit, a fine horse he would ride to the finish-line.

The parents stood to one side as the young woman went to work on Will's leg.

"What's your name? She asked.

"Willy-John, and this is my brother Thomas." He pointed in my direction.

"And what is your name?" he asked.

She poured him a tot of brandy, opened a drawer and removed a leather strap. "My name is Claire—here, bite down on this—it will help with the pain while I remove the bullet."

The projectile protruded from his skin on the underside of the hamstring. Willy-J didn't utter a word but his eyes showed the pain and a tear rolled down his cheek while she dug around in the wounded muscle.

"I cannot tell if the bone is broken or not," she said.

Willy-J murmured a few in-audible words, slurred by the brandy. He rarely drank liquor, unlike yours truly.

After the removal of the bullet she sloshed alcohol into the wound, proceeded to bandage the thigh and pulled the fabric tight, to make sure it didn't come loose. Will relaxed and spat the leather strap out onto the floor. Another tot of brandy passed hands to be chugged down in one gulp.

"You'll not be able to walk on that for at least two weeks."

I protested. "But we must get back to our regiment. Our Commanding officer will think we were killed by the marauding Boer party."

The farmer's wife spoke with a soft tone. "Don't worry about your army. The war I believe is almost over and you should be on your way home."

The rumors of the war's end rattled through the various British divisions on a regular basis but I had not heard it from the mouth of a Boer. If it held any truth, there could not be a better time for us to go back to England. I loved the military but conditions in South Africa proved far from congenial; to sleep in the open veld at night and wake in the mornings, almost rigid with frost, did not rate high on my list of entertainment. I'm not sure I would ever get used to it. Willy-J on the other hand seemed to be content with whatever situation he found himself in.

Shorter in stature than I, by a good two inches and broad at the shoulders with strong, muscular arms, Will could use himself in physical situations. I, on the other hand—tall, slim and in possession of a robust, athletic body, always provided him with back him up in times of trouble.

"I think your brother will sleep well tonight," said the young woman. I gave her a sheepish glance and held my tongue.

The farmer's wife spoke a few words in Afrikaans to her daughter, who left the room to fulfill a household chore.

"You can both sleep in Danie's office tonight. We will send word to your Kommandant to let him know you are safe."

Taken aback by the generous offer my question may have been laced with some cynicism.

"Why would you help us? We are your enemies. I think you have every right to hate us."

She placed her hands on hips, angled her head and fixed me with a stony stare. "We are not heathens. The Good Lord said we are to love our enemies and besides, here in the Cape the British have been good to the Afrikaners. We even have our own responsible government where we have been allowed by Lord Milner, to handle our own affairs. My husband and I often travel into Cape Town because Claire is studying to be a nurse. She is visiting us for a two-week break."

I must have looked a little embarrassed which caused her to smile. I wondered what she might come up with next but her husband returned from outside to hang his oil lantern on a hook near the kitchen door.

"It's time for us to turn in—we have a farm to run in the morning."

He looked at me. "You can undress in my office and give your clothes to my wife, Anna. We will get our house-servant to wash them for you—your brother's clothes as well."

I thanked them for their kindness and nurtured a notion: Willy-J and I had fallen with our backsides in the butter. With a candle in one hand I helped Will to his feet and half-carried him to the study where we removed our clothes. I placed the uniforms outside the door for the maid to retrieve in the morning. By the time I turned back into the room my brother's snores reverberated off the walls so, I blew out the candle and lay down next to him. The mattress felt lumpy and smelled of perspiration but to me it seemed like heaven. Within minutes I fell into a deep sleep.

∞∞

TWO

Love isn't something you find....
It's something that finds you. Loretta
Young.

The sunlight shone through the small window set high up in the outside wall. For a moment the room looked unfamiliar, before I turned my head to see Willy-J next to me with mouth wide open, a good imitation of a human, artesian well. I rolled over, stood to my feet and recounted the strange events of the previous evening, not sure what to do next. A peek out into the passageway followed. The lateness of the morning hour suggested a missed sunrise with its noisy accompaniment of farmyard roosters and the cackle of fowls.

A surprised Claire walked down the corridor from the opposite end and caught me half naked at the door. I ducked back into the room but not before I caught her, with hand clapped over mouth. Her attempt to stifle a shriek of laughter failed.

I slammed the door with vigor and woke Willy-John, who sat up, yawned and stretched out both his arms. "Blimey, Thomas. What're you up to—you'll wake the dead."

I saw no reason to explain my moment of embarrassment. "How's your leg?"

"It's really stiff but I'll survive."

"You really enjoyed the attentions of the young girl didn't you?"

He frowned. "What do you mean?"

"Any idiot could see you were utterly taken with her."

"Cum'ahn, get out of it, Thomas. You don't have a clue."

"I do so." I fluttered my eye-lashes.

"You're only twenty—you know nothing about love," he countered.

I gave him a cheeky grin. "As if the four years between us actually makes a difference? Except, you're more flabby around the middle than I am."

Will changed the subject. "Are the family up yet?"

"They've taken our clothes to wash and it sounds as though someone's busy with breakfast."

"Great, I'm famished, he said."

"Bet you can't wait to see her again."

He glared at me. "Who?"

"Florence Nightingale of course—who do you think, Chum—the tooth fairy?"

He held out a hand. "Help me up."

I stepped over the blanket and yanked him onto the good leg. He stood for a moment but an apparent loss of balance caused him to fall—I caught him in the nick of time.

"You'll not leave the bed for a while, William-John."

My words fell on deaf ears with Willy-J back in the arms of Morpheus again.

A knock on the door caught me off guard and sparked off a frantic search to find a cloth with which I could cover my nakedness. The blanket, draped over poor old Willy-J, came to light so I ripped it off him and flung it around my person.

"Just a minute," I shouted.

I cracked the door open to find an apologetic black woman with our washed and dried uniforms.

"Thank you, Ousie." I knew the Boers called their black women servants "Ousie," but had no clue as to what it meant.

She bowed and handed over the clothes which I took with a smile. A quick glance at Willy-J's trousers revealed a neat stitch job by a talented seamstress. I dressed and ventured out of the room toward the kitchen. A delightful smell of scrambled eggs, supplemented by the rich aroma of coffee, permeated the air. The farmer's wife fussed over various elements of the breakfast, her face a picture of concentration as she added ingredients with the aplomb of a chef. She turned her head to flash me a quick smile.

"You are the first soldiers to ever stay the night. We've had many pass through—agh, I'm so glad this war will soon end."

"Have you ever had Boer soldiers drop in at all?" I asked.

"From time to time—we have always helped anyone in need. The Good Lord requires it of us. Once a nice young man by the name of Denyse Reitz stopped by with four others—he said his father was the President of the Orange Free State. They were exhausted—chased by the British—poor things. I offered some soup we had on the stove but they did not even have time to finish it before they were off again."

I took it she didn't agree with all the demands the Boers required of their British occupiers. Much later I discovered the differences in attitude between the Boers of the Cape Colony verses those who supported the two republics.

"The Boers, here in the Cape Colony don't mind the British occupation and we can't see a successful outcome for the Boers in this war. The sooner it ends the better."

I smiled at her and sat down at the table. She poured a mug of coffee and pointed to a tin of condensed milk for a sweetener.

"Did you sleep well, Thomas?"

Uneasy at the use of my first name I wondered if the farmer might not set us up, to be handed over to the next party of Boer marauders, who might come for supplies.

"Yes thank you Mrs...I'm sorry, I was so tired last night I forgot to ask your surname.

"It's Beerman. Anna Beerman. My husband's name is Danie and our daughter is Claire."

The name Claire intrigued me. "Claire is not really an Afrikaans name is it?" I asked.

I am of French Huguenot descent. When my husband and I first married I still clung to my mother's culture and that's where my daughter's name comes from."

She placed a plate of scrambled eggs in front of me and I sat for a moment to savor the aroma. Since they appeared to be religious I bowed my head and pretended to pray.

"Thank you for your kindness," I said.

"How's your brother? Did he have a good night?" She asked.

"I think so—he seems a little weak this morning but I'm sure once he has eaten breakfast he'll be fine."

"That leg will require a lot of rest and he needs to be careful when he puts weight on it."

"Your daughter seems to know a lot about medical matters."

"She is doing a nurse's diploma at the new Stellenbosch University in Cape Town and often helps out in the local hospital between classes."

"We have much to thank you and your family for."

"Do not worry about it, Thomas. The Good Lord states in the Bible we must all love our enemies. The real enemy is Satan, who makes us hate each other, but my husband and I do not hate the British."

Claire entered and sat at the table opposite me.

With washed face, combed hair a new dress she looked a different person.

"You look very nice this morning." I said.

"A little better than you did earlier," she giggled.

I blushed and looked at my plate. "I didn't have any clothes to put on."

She laughed and I felt a sudden affinity with her. In the dull light of the lantern, on the previous evening, her face appeared dowdy but this morning in the natural sunlight she looked quite beautiful.

A sound caught our attention followed by the appearance of a figure in the doorway. A self-conscious Willy-John stood there. Decked out in the uniform with uncombed hair and stubbly chin, he presented a mixture of Knight in armor and a disheveled Quixote, beaten up by one of the windmills.

I jumped up to the rescue, for fear he would fall if he took another step, but Claire beat me to it. She grabbed him around the waist to provide support.

"You shouldn't be up, Sir." Her politeness took me by surprise and I laughed.

"I haven't heard anyone call him, Sir, ever."

"My name's William. Please call me, Will," said Willy-J.

They looked into each other's eyes. I'd lived with my brother all my life and I never saw a similar look like pass between him and any other woman.

*

And so, with the cupid's arrow buried in Willy-J's heart the rest, as they say, is history.

The war ended two days later and the British forces demobilized. We stayed with the Beerman family for another two weeks until Willy-J could use a cane to move around. Claire doctored and nursed him the entire time—the two became inseparable. I wanted to get home but my brother did not want to leave for obvious reasons. Their love for each other reached demonstrative proportions, which often caused me to leave the room in acute embarrassment whenever they kissed or stared into each other's eyes.

Mr. and Mrs. Beerman appeared tolerant of the relationship but I envisaged an end to it at some point. Our mother's last letter begged us both to call it a day and come home. She knew nothing of Will's romance.

I managed to twist his ear a few times.

"We need to go home, Will. Mother is longing to see us again and so are the others."

"I know, Thomas. The problem is Claire and I are in love—I can't just leave her."

"You can return when things are more settled here," I argued.

"But Claire and I couldn't stand to be parted for even a day—you don't understand, Thomas."

In the end he relented but swore he would return at the earliest opportunity. Claire, still with a year of studies left decided Will should travel to England, see his family and return at a later time.

South Africa's future path, now to be underwritten by the British Empire, stood at a crossroad. The creation of turmoil amongst the Afrikaners due to the annexation of the two Republics became evident to all. After the treaty of Vereeniging there remained little need for us to hang around and we booked our passage to Britain.

A tearful good bye followed at the docks as we boarded the mail boat for a ten-day sail back to England. Willy-J remained quiet throughout the entire return trip and I knew life for us would never be the same again.

The family waited to greet us while we disembarked and I felt a sense of sadness grip me. Although all still looked familiar, the town of Margate no longer felt like the home we knew before the war. I guess both Willy-J and I suffered a maturation of sorts—perhaps a little before our time.

If I thought we might fit back into the English way of life my naivety may never have known any bounds, but the truth is England no longer offered the home awareness we once knew.

∞∞

THREE

Every new beginning comes from some other beginning's end. —Seneca

"She's pregnant".

"What?" My dismay soared with sudden astonishment.

"I said, she is pregnant."

"Who the devil are you talking about, Willy-J?"

"Claire."

I stared at my brother with wide open eyes. "You sure?"

"Her letter—she's pregnant." He stared at me in consternation and dropped the two pages of a letter, which fluttered to the ground.

"Oh crikey—this throws a spanner in the works," I said.

"I have to go back—I can't leave her there alone."

"She has her parents who can take care of her."

Willy-J looked at me with resignation. "Her dad has become ill and they don't know what's wrong with him."

The wind, taken out of my sails, left me without suggestions.

"What are you going to do, Will?"

"I'm through here. She's all I've been thinking about ever since we returned. I must go back to South Africa."

"But, what will you do?"

"Get a job, moron."

"You going to tell Mom?"

"Of course—tonight."

Willy-J worked with a local carpentry firm as a journeyman and although he earned an above average wage he could never settle down. He spoke often of a plan to bring Claire to Kent but she felt it not expedient to leave her studies for a life in England. Now, with her father's illness, she might be even more reluctant to leave her home.

"With a child on the way it might mess up her education—I must go and help."

To argue the point appeared fruitless.

"I will not be going with you," I said.

He looked at me and for a moment and I saw his shoulders relax. "Tom, you are your own man. Maybe it's time for us to part ways, but I'll miss you."

I could see the tears in his eyes. To Leave Britain permanently presented certain difficulties, but to leave your brother—much harder.

At home all hell broke loose. Mom didn't take the news well, called Willy-J all sorts of names and maligned Claire—I drew the line. My mother knew little about Claire. The little she knew she gleaned from our conversations.

"You can't make rash judgments like that, Mother—you've never met her. If it's anyone's fault its mine. I failed to talk sense into my brother's head when he lay on a mattress in their home, wounded and vulnerable. But it's done now and let nothing more be said about the matter."

My words shocked mother and she sobbed for hours. I felt for her and could have bitten my tongue but no one talks bad about my brother or Claire, without the benefit of my anger. After a while she calmed down and thought better of the whole incident. Willy-J did not say a word—I admired his patience.

Later he sat down next to her. "Mom, I'm sorry to have upset you. I know you have only just got us back and here I am, off again. But what Thomas said is true; what's done is done. Let's all make the best of it."

Mother dabbed at her eyes with a handkerchief. "I worry so much about you boys. Your father had more control over you when he was alive."

The next morning Will booked his passage to South Africa and arranged for all his assets to be sold. He gave me the address of the bank the money should be wired to and I promised to uphold my end.

"Look after Mom, Thomas—she's fragile."

I promised to do my best. Will's ship, one of the old Union Castle mail-ships, left the following Thursday from South Hampton and he slipped away before any of the family could say goodbye. He left a letter, which I delivered by hand, to mother and the others. Mother did not speak of him or Claire again and I understood how hard it must have been for her to lose her oldest son for a second time.

Two years later my job took me to the top of a high smoke stack with a beautiful view, which overlooked the whole of Margate. While at work on a cold day in the spring of 1904, snowflakes swirled down around my friend and I as we prepared to lay the last few bricks on the chimney's top perimeter. With a sudden epiphany I realized my heart no longer belonged to England.

Willy-J's letters, filled with praise for the new South Africa plus his life with Claire and their young son, William, created, within the confines of my dull existence, a penchant for adventure. I missed my brother and the excitement of the many escapades we endured in our far-away land. My allegiance to the great British Empire no longer imparted the same sense of honor and duty for me as it did in previous times.

With the last brick laid in completion of the stack perimeter I threw my trowel down the cavernous hole and proclaimed, "That's the last brick I'll ever lay in England."

My colleague looked surprised. "Lost your mind, Tom?"

I gazed over the panoramic view of the town. "No, I've not lost it —I have only just found it."

I hated to leave my mother and the other family members but every young man, at some time in his life, needs to leave the nest for the good of everyone. I believed mother suspected it all along for she took my news with calm resignation when I broached the subject. The next day, I wrote Willy-J a short note and booked my ticket to Cape Town, then gathered up my belongings to sell them.

I can say in my defense—when others have said Thomas Satherwaite is a fun-lover who knows how to spend money—the converse of the latter in reference to money, is also true. I know how to save and my account at the local bank reflected it. Will taught me a good principle—a rainy day will come, so make sure you prepare well for it.

On a Thursday morning in the spring of 1904, I boarded a Union Castle Line steamer for the journey to my new home and the commencement of the most eventful saga of my life.

∞∞

FOUR

....it's time to start something new and trust the magic of beginnings. —Meister Eckhart.

Spring in South Africa ushered in a seasonal nostalgia of fragrant flowers and sounds of a vibrant, indigenous birdlife.

Cape Town, a magical city endowed with theatres and hotels, dress shops and tailor shops, attracted an eclectic mix of rich and poor. Willy-John and Claire lived in a middle-class district in South Cape Town with Claire's mother. Her father had succumbed to tuberculosis a year prior to my arrival at which time Claire's mother sold the farm off to a neighbor.

Willy-J chose to leave his trade as a carpenter, after the offer of a job in the local Police force and on my arrival, we celebrated his recent promotion to sergeant. I joined him in the force and it augured well for the two of us. The adaption of our military experience to crime resolution made us a formidable team and we terrorized the many small-time criminals in our district. Within months I received a promotion to sergeant and Willy-J to Staff-sergeant, but several months later he pulled me aside.

"I've heard that the government is looking for young men who want to develop land. I've been thinking—"

I could have waxed prophetic and told him I knew his thoughts on the matter but instead I let him spit it out.

"I've been thinking, little brother. We should look into it—try our hand at farming, I mean?"

"Life becoming too tame for you?" I asked.

"You know me—I need more excitement. This job's okay but it's pretty repetitive."

"I'm, with you in whatever you decide. What about Claire?"

"I'm sure she'll jump at the opportunity. Farming's in her blood. We have some money and it's time for us to dream a little bigger than this."

To emphasize the point he stretched out a hand and swung it around in an arc.

"What's the deal?" I asked.

"The Government offers a ninety-nine year lease on ground between Pietersburg and Louis Trichardt—it's bushveld, full of wild game and there's opportunity to farm dairy or crops."

"We know nothing about farming," I complained.

"I spoke to Jan Duplessis, the guy who works in the main office—he said there were plenty of opportunities besides the farming of ground. The road from Pietersburg is the main route to Beit Bridge and Rhodesia. He says more and more wagon trains are making the trip and there are few shops in between."

"Are you thinking of opening a butchery or something like that?"

"Jan said if we get in now the lease on the ground is still cheap but it will become more expensive when more people get involved."

"What are we waiting for then? Let's go talk to Claire."

I loved it when Willy-John exercised his penchant for business. He did have some experience, gained in his youth. After my father's death my mother, on her own, struggled to run the family boarding house in Margate and Willy-J, fifteen years old, helped her on the weekends. He developed better systems for the enterprise and continued to do this throughout his carpentry apprenticeship, until the British military signed him up in 1899.

With the shift over I felt a tinge of excitement as we caught the bus back to the suburb where Will and Claire lived. My stay in Cape Town might be shorter than I expected and I loved the idea of farm life. The drier climate in the Northern Province, closer to the equator, offered better conditions for chest ailments, from which Willy-J suffered on occasions.

Later, the four of us sat around the small fire in the living-room. Claire, like Will and I, longed for greater excitement but Anna, who still mourned the loss of her husband, appeared hesitant about the idea. Farm-life, however, posed a much greater attraction than the city.

Willy-J promised to obtain more details from the local government office in the morning and with the idea fixed in our minds we called it a night. Under normal circumstances sleep comes with ease but the prospect of the new adventure took over and I lay awake for hours.

*

The next morning we left for work as usual. Claire, with young William now twenty months old, waved goodbye to us as they sat on the verandah in the sunshine. Claire's mother, Anna, remained in her bedroom until ten every morning. She helped with the general housework and looked after William while Claire busied herself in the garden.

Willy-J took some time off to visit the local government office. Neither of us knew much about the Northern Province other than summertime tended to be hot and dry. I still entertained an air of excitement, vision and fantasy——we would become millionaires, or so I thought. Will's words to me−to be careful what I wished for−never entered my mind.

We sat on the bench outside the Police Station, under the Soap Dogwood near the front entrance, to eat our lunch and discuss the details of our proposed venture. The town rested in quiet anticipation for the night-life to begin. The deviousness of the underworld always stirred in the night-hours; a lot depended on the shift we worked but the practice of crime, both petty and bold, thrived under the cloak of darkness.

Willy-J unwrapped his sandwich and leaned forward to talk.

"Found out quite a bit this morning."

I waited for him to elaborate.

"The area holding the most promise is Kweetsa. It's close to a small town by the name of Louis Trichardt and the government is offering huge parcels of ground for lease, from as little as twenty-seven pound sterling per annum."

"So what's at this Kweetsa," I asked.

"It's a water-hole fed by a spring and is situated where the road between Pietersburg and Beit Bridge is intersected by the trail from Tzaneen. Travelers can stop to refresh their oxen and the road hosts a lot of wagon-train traffic."

"Are there no shops or homesteads?" I asked.

"There is only one shop run by a woman from a nearby town, called Louis Trichardt, where a few more shops exist. The agent told me if we opened some shops in Kweetsa we could make a killing on the pass-through trade."

"Who supplies the shop there?"

"The owners supply it from their main shop in Louis Trichardt but apparently it's always running out of goods and only stays open for a few days in the week. The person running it travels from Louis Trichardt where she and her husband have a larger business."

"So when do we leave?"

"I need to talk to Claire and Anna first—it could be as soon as the end of the month."

"Suits me fine, brother," I said.

At the end of our shift we made our way home by bus, in discussion of the pros and cons of the plan. Later, around dinner, everyone agreed to the move. Claire and Anna, concerned by the danger involved in police work and spurred on by the bonus of a return to farm life, found peace with the venture. Claire made one request—her piano would accompany us and be stored in Pretoria until Willy-John and I completed the farmhouse we planned to build.

I argued the move of such a heavy instrument over the distance but Willy-J felt she needed to continue with her music. The train ride turned out to be a bore for me. Willy-J and Claire, on the other hand, found much of interest along the way to occupy their attention. Anna kept herself busy with young William and acted as his nanny for the entire duration of the trip which took seven days to complete.

The metropolis of Pretoria held little fascination for us and we didn't stay long. With the piano offloaded and placed in a storage facility the family spent one night in a cheap hotel where we struggled to sleep due to the noise from an adjacent saloon. The next morning Will negotiated a ride by ox- wagon to Kweetsa.

I breathed a sigh of relief when we left the noisy crowds and shops behind for the quietness of the bushveld. The constant creak and groan of the ox-wagon with its wooden wheels, accompanied by the whistle and sharp crack of the young voorlooper's whip, broke the stillness of the open plains.

The 'voorlooper'—or young boy who walked in front of the oxen belonged to our black wagon-driver, a large Zulu man with a weather-beaten face, bloodshot eyes and bad teeth. The two latter ailments resulted from a cannabis-type weed called Dagga, which many of the black folk smoked.

Willy-J purchased a horse in Pretoria and spent his day astride the animal, a fine specimen he called, "The Colonel." Claire and Anna, who travelled with young Will in her arms for most of the way, sat on the wagon behind the driver and myself.

At night we slept in a tent while the driver and his voorlooper bedded down under the stars around the fire. Everyone took a turn at night to watch for wild animals, which became more numerous the further North we travelled.

The rainy season of September started halfway through the journey with a formidable downpour. At one point the deluge threatened to engulf the wagon and the voorlooper, who stopped the train and scurried to get beneath the wagon. We followed and must have made a laughable sight, all huddled together between the wheels. The poor oxen stood with their heads down and endured the storm's fury.

When it passed over we all popped out from our place of refuge with much laughter. Our clothes soon dried out with the immediate appearance of the sun from behind the huge overhead, cumulous clouds. We continued along the bumpy trail, the main road between Pretoria and Pietersburg, with stops every three hours to rest the oxen.

At each stop we stretched ourselves out on the short grass next to the wagon to relieve the stiffness in our muscles and spoke about expectations. Our driver, Simon, a Zulu by birth regaled us with bushveld stories and escapades from his youth while he puffed on a dagga cigarette he called a "Zol". The more he smoked the wilder the stories.

The journey from Pretoria to Pietersburg took us two weeks and by the time we arrived at Kweetsa four days later, everyone knew all about travelling on an ox-wagon and life in the bush.

∞∞

FIVE

Destiny is not a matter of chance. It is a matter of choice... — William Jennings Bryan

On arrival we disembarked the wagon to explore our new home. Willy-J stopped outside the store, a converted barn at the base of the kopje, the landmark upon which the community derived its name. The storekeeper, a woman by the name of Mrs. Brink, told him her husband ran a business in Louis Trichardt and she travelled to Kweetsa every Tuesday to open the store and stay over until Thursday. Alongside the barn stood a rough stable for horses and a room for wagon drivers to sleep in. These drivers, often black men in the employ of merchants who supplied their wears to the Louis Trichardt, Messina and the Beit Bridge areas, fended for themselves. Many wagon trains appeared to be families on the move from one place to another, plus horse-riders out on the hunt.

She disparaged the local black population as polite but lazy, and not worthy of employment.

"Only a few want to work and are reliable. They are mostly cattle farmers and thieves," she said.

I raised my eyebrows at her attitude but realized it is how many of the Afrikaans farmers spoke. Willy-J and I did not have any real experience with the native people but we soon learned about their culture. In time, we found the Northern Sotho to be the best employees, followed by the few Zulus. The others didn't want to work for the white people and lived in their kraals, where they farmed a few crops and drank lots of home-made beer.

Mrs. Brink took out a rough, home-drawn map and placed it on the counter while we enjoyed some cups of coffee and pancakes, which she offered for a small price. The map turned out to be one similar to the one supplied us by the government office in Cape Town.

"You are the first to rent land here. There are not many people who want to farm anymore. Most, like my husband and I, have moved to small towns like Trichardt because it is peaceful. Many have left for the big cities to find work but we decided to start a business and bring up our kids, away from the bad influences."

She pointed out a track adjacent to the barn, told us to follow it for five hundred paces and look for the main survey beacon, on the right-hand side. Willy-J's instructions from the agent, to start at the main survey beacon and use the legend on the map to work out the coordinates of our leased property, gelled with Mrs. Brink's explanation.

We left the shop, walked down the path and paced out five hundred yards to the main beacon. Our property stretched for miles, more than we could ever use and the land, level with a few small kopjes dotted around, supported a host of different shrub and tree types.

The driver outspanned the oxen and we off-loaded all the small items first. Willy-J chopped down a small tree to rig up two poles on which the bigger, heavier cases could slide off the back of the wagon to the ground.

The two military bell-tents purchased in Pretoria, needed a patch of ground cleared for their setup and I chose a spot next to a tall tree, about twenty yards from the beacon. The tents became our official home for the foreseeable future, until Willy-J and I found the time to build the main residence. Night fell and two lanterns hung from the tree branches to give us enough light to finish the set up. Earlier, Mrs. Brink accompanied by her black body guard with an old military rifle in one hand, rode off on their horses in the direction of Trichardt, a distance of about twenty-five miles.

Brave woman, I thought to myself. I walked off to gather firewood from an old, dead tree I saw about one hundred yards along a path which must have been made by local blacks. Ten minutes later I returned with enough branches to feed a fire through the night. The driver collected a host of small rocks to form a small enclosure for my short branches to be stacked up against each other and Claire produced some old newspaper for a fire-starter.

Bully-beef, mixed with beans, topped the menu and we all ate a hearty meal. The driver and his son slept on the back of the wagon under a make-shift tent while the four of us snuggled down under blankets in one of the bell-tents. We stored all our food supplies and ammunition for the rifles in the second bell-tent—we already felt at home— Kweetsa's newest residents.

*

Out first night and the days to follow, will always be imprinted on my memory with indelible perpetuity. The next morning I found the sunrise to be the most unforgettable of experiences. The birdlife and insects formed a remarkable symphony.

The beautiful orange, yellow color of the sky painted a picture of pristine purity underwritten by the fresh dew, like a tarp flung over the grass and bushes. I became as a creature of the veld, in unity and a connectedness to nature.

The weeks passed and turned into months. We busied ourselves with the general purpose of life, built a rough homestead and ploughed up ground to plant vegetables.

One day our neighbor, Mrs. Brink fell from her horse while on her way home and her black guard came to ask us for help. The poor woman broke her pelvis and we feared for her life, but she survived the ordeal. The shop closed up and she never returned. After a month her husband came to see us and offered the barn with its contents for a very reasonable price. We jumped at the opportunity and our dream of business got off the ground.

*

Six months later Willy-J and I completed the Main rooms of our homestead. I made bricks out of clay, baked by the summer sun and constructed the roof from tree timbers and grass thatch. We also built a new barn to house the horses and three cows purchased from the local village, situated on our leased property, about three miles from the homestead. Up to this time our existence relied upon the hunt for venison, milk from the cows and home-grown vegetables, but when winter came the morning frosts destroyed the contents of the garden. The Kweetsa farm grew in the number of its domestic animals; after ten months we owned four cows, two oxen and three horses and learned to plant vegetables for each season.

About sixty black locals, all Sothos, lived in the small village on our land, close by—their continued presence a condition as stipulated in our contract. It allowed the indigenous people of the region to live in their original kraals without any interference. This turned out to be a good arrangement because it stimulated our trade and the growth of black consciousness for products developed by whites. The black folk lived on milk, meat from their cattle, homemade beer, and mielie-meal; all other supplement to their diet came by compliments of the white people's industry.

The village also supplied a steady stream of men who worked on the development of crops and vegetables. Mrs. Brink's assessment of the workforce proved correct to a degree. Many worked for half-a-day and disappeared after lunch. I did, however, find one man who seemed eager to earn his wage, a youngster of twenty-three, Polo by name.

Polo and I became good friends despite the differences in status and education I found him in possession of a useful bush-knowledge, which helped me on the trips to hunt venison. I learned about all the different types of game, where they could be found, how to stalk them plus bush protocol.

Willy-J spent most of his time in the store and often rode into Louis Trichardt to get essential supplies. The wagon trains became more frequent with new factories in Pietersburg and a lot of folk traveled through to Trichardt on weekends.

Five years later we added two more stores and a hostel with an adjacent saloon to accommodate travelers. With the help of Polo and a few of his cronies from the village I managed all the construction. These good times typified bushveld life and when I look back now, I realize how idyllic the situation turned out to be. Every Friday I rode my horse into Louis Trichardt and visited with various women, often to spend the night and return to Kweetsa the next morning, with a hangover.

Willy-J and Claire often took me aside to read the riot act.

"You need to be more responsible Thomas. It's very dangerous to ride the trail at night—especially when you're drunk."

"But my horse knows the way home," I countered.

I understood their anxiety. They depended on me to be the hunter and the builder and worried I might end up dead in a Trichardt bar one night. Business and the general quality of our life, however, improved.

One day a new potential for Kweetsa materialized with the arrival of a railroad survey team. The railway Line Extension Committee from Pretoria now set its sights on Beit Bridge within two years and our little enclave of shops chosen to be a future terminus became a water intake point. We could not have been happier.

Claire found an indulgence of her own. She spent a few days in Pietersburg one year in search of clothes for the children and came across a shop with two large Great Danes on the porch. She asked the owner if anyone bred the dogs and expressed a wish to purchase a puppy.

"Yes my dear. In fact we have three pups at home, two months old and two of them must be sold." To cut a long story short Claire came home with two Great Dane pups, a male and a female.

Willy-J took to the dogs and felt sure they could be bred for an income.

"After what you paid for these animals, we have to sell Great Danes one day, Love. Just think—a Kweetsa Pet shop."

She laughed. "I can't see you looking after six-week old pups, darling."

With a train-stop planned for Kweetsa, Willy-J drew up plans for additions to the hostel and we named it the Kweetsa Hotel. A year later business increased and I could say with pride, we became quite wealthy. Our fortunes flourished with an added bonus—a geological survey discovered a useful mineral on the farm—corundum, a hard crystal-like rock, used in abrasives and emery material. I often wondered about the greyish rocks but never once thought they may contain a valuable substance. Willy-John could not have been more ecstatic.

But then matters took a dramatic turn.

∞∞

SIX

Some people come into our lives and leave footprints on our hearts... —Flavia.

On Tuesday the 8th October, 1912, Willy-J visited a friend in Louis Trichardt, the owner of a stable of fine horses. I'm not sure if he intended to buy a new horse but flush with money and with several fillies on sale Will decided to buy. With the deal done on a handshake Willy-J rode out of Trichardt on his acquisition, plus a brand new saddle to boot.

The three hour ride back to Kweetsa gave him an opportunity to evaluate the filly, which appeared to possess the character of a wild mustang. I know Willy-J enjoyed the raw strength of spirited mounts and gave little heed for his own safety while out on a ride. A friend told me later he saw horse and rider pass by the new railway terminus at a fierce gallop and come to an abrupt stop in a cloud of dust outside our newest shop, a farm implement and service center. Later, the shop's proprietor mentioned a discussion on aspects of the lease agreement, which took place over a cup of coffee before Will, eager to show Claire the new horse, left for home. Another shop owner saw

Willy-J mount up and ride out at a fast canter to-ward the farm house.

On arrival at the tether-rail in front of the ve-randah Will stood up on the stirrup to disembark his mount and Claire, who heard his approach, walked out to greet her husband. The two boister-ous, Great Dane pups also charged out in joyous enthusiasm and jumped up at the horse while Will, still in the process of his dismount, tried to shoo them away.

The new horse, un-accustomed to dogs took fright, shied away and dislodged the unfortunate Willy-J. As Claire watched in horror the horse took off with her husband's foot still caught up in the stirrup and no chance to recover his balance. The horse galloped off toward the cattle Kraal and dragged Will's body over the bumpy surface. His shoulders and head bounced like a football on the bumpy terrain, over a distance of four hundred yards, before the filly came to a stop.

With a high-pitched scream Claire followed at a run. On arrival at the spot she knelt down to cradle Willy-J's heavily fractured cranium in her hands, but too late to be of any help. With a sob she enveloped him with her arms and held the broken body to her bosom. He survived for a few more minutes before the dreadful wounds took him from this world.

Claire told me all this afterwards; she felt so helpless, and blamed herself for lack of control over the dogs—it would have saved his life, she said.

I arrived on the scene ten minutes after the fact. Later, we sat in the lounge together surrounded by our friends, some who rented shops and others who worked for us, all who lived in the small community of Kweetsa.

I looked at Claire, slumped in her chair, still in shock and unbelief. Her tear-stained cheeks and red eyes told the story of her grief. I realized it wrong to lay blame at anyone's door.

"You couldn't have known the dogs would react like that," I said.

She looked down at her hands, folded on her lap. "The dogs always ran out to greet Will—they loved him. 'The Colonel' never shied because he knew the dogs well, but this new animal—," she trailed off and dabbed at her eyes with a handkerchief.

"We must make arrangements for the funeral," said Willem Cronje, the man who worked as the bartender in the saloon and supervised the hotel kitchen.

"There is much to be done but let's leave it until the morning," I answered.

By nine o'clock all the empathizers left for their homes and the homestead rested in quiet morbidity. The house felt so empty without Will.

I turned to Claire. "You'd better turn in. We'll have a lot to do tomorrow and much to discuss."

She stood and shuffled off to the bedroom and a long night lay ahead for both of us—my mind could not accept the fact of my brother's death. Our lives at Kweetsa would never be the same again.

Most nights, before bed, Will and I often indulged ourselves in a nightcap. The kitchen cabinet contained all our supplies plus a bottle of Brandy which contained about three tots in it. I took the bottle and moved out to a chair on the verandah for some fresh air. The brandy brought some consolation to the end of a bad day and before long I fell asleep in the chair. I didn't wake up until four am in the morning—once again, the awful truth of Will's death, came to mind and I slunk off to my bedroom in despair.

The funeral took place four days later, on a Saturday, with some cherished moments of our life history shared at the service. Claire's mother, Anna asked the minister of the church she attended in Pietersburg, to take the service. I braced myself to share the eulogy but my effort gave way to tears before I could complete it. Claire sat through the event with stoic patience but detached frame of mind and God knows what thoughts she entertained. After the service all the guests congregated at the house where we shared coffee, tea and cake together. By late afternoon everyone departed to their homes in somber silence. Claire retired to her bedroom and I to mine—our Sotho housemaid,

Letsatsi, asked if we required our usual evening meal but I declined—she cleaned up the lounge and returned to the village.

The next day Claire and I saddled up two horses for a ride to Louis Trichardt. I am not an atheist but I also don't have any firm religious convictions. Claire, on the other hand, attended a service at the Reformed Church in Trichardt on occasion. We both thought it to be a good diversion from the awfulness of a Sunday, spent in silence around the farmhouse, with the memory of Willy-John everywhere.

Later in the day after our return from Trichardt, Claire and I sat on the verandah with a cup of coffee. We gazed across the veld, lost in our own thoughts, when out of the blue she spoke for the first time since the evening of Willy-J's death.

"You blame me, don't you?"

Taken aback I hesitated. The hesitation gave away some of my built up anger. Deep down I felt she shouldered some culpability.

"Don't be silly," I lied. "You are not to blame."

"But you think I should have controlled the dogs—stopped them from rushing down the steps—don't you?"

I gave the matter some thought. "I could say I should have been there to stop the horse from bolting—the point is, Claire, nobody can be held accountable for Will's death. It was just a terrible accident."

"Should I get rid of the dogs?" she asked.

Again, I hesitated. "The dogs did what they always do. They have no understanding of any different behavior and the horse had only been broken in a week before the accident. Besides, I doubt whether Will would have blamed anyone."

She remained quiet for a while and we sipped on our mugs of coffee. I felt the urge for a cigarette so I stood to walk into the lounge, where the packet and matches lay on the table. Claire's eyes appeared glazed and unfocused.

"I can't stay here anymore," she said.

Her words hit me like a train.

"You can't stay here anymore because you think I blame you for his death?"

"Not really. I can't stay here anymore because there are too many memories. I am going to move to my mother's place in Pietersburg for a while."

Claire's mother, Anna, moved to Pietersburg two years before to join with a man she met while on a search for new clothes. The two, lonesome and in their sixties, yearned for a relationship. She felt Claire didn't need her as a babysitter anymore as several black women, from the village, looked after the two boys and one girl—William, aged nine, Robert, five years and Shirley, four. Claire celebrated her thirtieth birthday six months before Will's demise. Young and attractive, with a good future no shortage of suiters in the Province, existed.

Unable to find words with which to counter her decision I moved off into the lounge to retrieve my smokes. In retrospect, Claire's move prevented the community from frivolous talk about the two of us with one caveat—I would miss her assistance in the businesses.

After six months, an on-off courtship of a girl from Louis Trichardt made it difficult for me to be under the same roof with my sister-in-law. Olivia Potgieter and I talked marriage from time to time but made no firm decision to tie the knot.

Olivia's father owned a dairy farm outside Louis Trichardt. A well-respected family in the community they exemplified the traditional way of farm life. She, like Claire descended from Boer stock on her father's side but her mother came from Scotland. I moved back out to the verandah to puff on my cigarette.

"It will be better for all of us," she said.

"The farm is your home too, Claire."

"I know but it contains so much of Willy-John—I believe I should make a clean break."

"Perhaps it's for the best," I said.

She walked to the front door and stopped. "I'm off to bed now. We can discuss it again in the morning. I will take my piano."

"You must take whatever you need," I said.

She turned and left.

My head spun around in circles. My grief still needed to vent and with sudden emotion I choked up. I felt anger in my heart—anger at the world because Will's departure came far too soon for any of us—anger at a God who allowed it to happen. I sat in the chair for a few hours with my head buried in shaky hands while all the memories of our passed escapades paraded through my mind. Will had helped me out of many difficult situations and it dawned on me—his future influence in my life relied now on my memory of his fraternal tutorship.

The hotel and other businesses, all overseen by Will and Claire cluttered the inbox of my responsibilities, to stare at me like fish in a bowl. My forte lay in the construction of shops and abodes, farm work and the hunt for venison. I knew squat about finances and little about management. Will even told me what to plant on the farm and when—he understood everything about the enterprises because he provided the initial know-how. What would I do without him? Even Claire knew more than I did.

With a heavy heart I decided to head for bed but the silence of my room offered no solace. It sufficed to say the next day found me troubled and argumentative due to an extreme lack of sleep. At breakfast I asked Claire to call in on the businesses, check each one's status and prepare the managers for my oversight. Claire agreed to check on the businesses for the last time.

"We can come to an agreement to split the profits," she said.

"I'll talk about that when I get back from the hunt, I'm taking Polo with me."

∞∞

SEVEN

Grace is free sovereign favor to the ill-deserving... *—B.B. Warfield.*

The day turned out to be a hot one. Polo and I decided to make for a natural spring of water which we often used on the hunt. The path led passed a black-gray, colored rocky outcrop, said to contain the corundum mineral, cause of the surveyor's enthusiasm. I made a mental note to follow up on the potential project; it occurred to me I would now be called upon to make decisions for the potential Mine operation.

On arrival at the spring I knelt down to quench my thirst and fill the water bottle. Polo climbed to the top of the outcrop and sat down on the biggest rock where he kept an eye out for game and chewed on a piece of grass. The base of the outcrop served as a natural outlet for the spring and provided a steady stream of cool water which fed a tiny rock-pool, almost hidden by the long veld grass.

With my attention focused on the small spout of water with which I hoped to quench my thirst, I failed to see the grass movement a few feet off to the left. Rocky outcrops provided a host of places for predators to hide and any lapse in caution while on a rest-stop could have serious consequences.

A sudden movement in the grass revealed a large African Rock Python about to lunge at what it thought might be a rock-rabbit or 'dassie', as the Afrikaners call them. Pythons are well known for taking down medium sized buck and I should have known better than to be caught off guard. The python moved with lightning speed to take my shoulder in its jaws and flung the long, reticulate body over my waist. The tail remained out of sight, anchored to an unseen rock—no time for me to react.

I screamed in fear as the pain of the bite immobilized my arm. The power and impetus, generated by the animal's weight, flung me over onto my back and the long, muscular body coiled and tightened around mine as we rolled in the long grass. Polo gaped with unbelief at the sight and got such a fright he slipped off his rocky perch to land in the grass on his knees. It took several moments before he realized my dire predicament.

The python's immense muscular strength tightened the coils with death-grip intensity, to press the air out of my lungs with every constriction. I could do little with both arms trapped at my side and we thrashed around for what felt like an eternity. In sudden realization of my plight Polo jumped up and rushed to my assistance. The rifle lay against a large rock close by but fear of in-

jury to me prevented its use. One option remained—the knife he carried on his belt.

I could feel the breath in my lungs diminish
every time the snake constricted and a dreadful
panic seized my mind. With the beast's tail anchored, the strongest of men would not be able to
resist the force exerted by the coils and I felt my
lungs begin to fail. Polo pulled the knife from his
belt and jumped onto my back in search of the
python's head. The jaws, still attached to my
shoulder, clamped even tighter as he tried to get
one hand around the neck in an attempt to pry the
head upwards and position the knife against its
throat. This proved impossible so he hacked away
behind, at the back of the cranium and the snake
eased off constriction of coils to address the new
threat. Seconds before, I must have been close to
death because I saw my family parade before my
eyes. Willy-J smiled and beckoned to me while my
mother looked on with a sadness and tearful eyes.

All of a sudden the python's body relaxed and
air flowed back into my deflated lungs. Through
the murkiness of my re-instatement I could hear
Polo's gratitude as he gave thanks to God his
Morena had not died.

With the ordeal over I lay against a rock and
regained my strength. I could not help but marvel
at my friend. Sothos are born naturalists and they
will not kill an animal without a valid reason. The
python's death lay in the virtue of a life

saved—mine. We remained at the spring for another hour before I felt strong enough to walk again. I still needed to shoot a buck for the larder.

Polo asked if he could come back later and take the remains of the python home. I never considered snake meat to be a delicacy but the black folk entertained no such capriciousness.

The rest of the day turned out to be quite lucrative. We came across a stembuck feeding at the edge of a line of mimosa trees and one shot with the Mauser brought it down. These buck are inclined to wander away from their group and I have often seen them on their own. Polo picked up the carcass and slung it across his broad shoulders for transport to the outcrop where we encountered the python. To carry the buck home rested with me. The snake's body measured at least thirty feet. In an attempt to shoulder the full weight of the carcass he found it too heavy and settled for the thickest section, near the middle. I could still feel the pain of the bite on my shoulder—my ribs felt as though one or two might have been bruised but like a true martyr, I lifted the stembuck onto my shoulders. A treat awaited the villagers—not only the shared meat but the story of the incident. Polo saved my life and it would never be forgotten.

Evening fell with slow but progressive determination as I struggled along the path with the buck across my shoulders. When I trudged up to the stairs of the verandah, Claire jumped up to lend some assistance. My strength gave in on the first step. I fell to my knees and remained there while she placed her arms around me in an effort to support my weight. Her body, soft and warm against my arm felt good at first but awkwardness overcame me. I flung the buck off my shoulders and regained my balance to push past her. She let go of me and stepped back.

"I didn't mean to—," she gasped.

"Don't worry—I've had a harrowing day."

She helped me carry the buck to the shed where I hung it from one of the rafters. We moved into the kitchen where Claire placed a pot of coffee on the old wood-fired stove.

I collapsed onto a kitchen chair and opened the neck of my bush-shirt to expose the snake-bite wound. She saw the congealed blood and puncture marks.

"Oh my God, Thomas—what happened?"

I related the incident of the python attack. "I'm over it now."

Claire burrowed underneath the sink, to come up with a bowl and a cloth. She decanted some warm water into the bowl and cleaned up the wound.

"You are very lucky—you could have been killed. I hope you'll reward Polo for saving you."

"I will, in my way," I answered. "It's just accepted that we help one another when in the bush. The next time I could be saving his life."

She applied some antiseptic which stung like the devil. "That should stop any infection," She said.

"Thank you."

She smiled wanly. "We need to talk about the businesses."

"I know. I have just felt at such a loss—I don't really know what to do," I said.

"It has been a very sudden loss for all of us. Will has left a huge void."

We sat and sipped our coffees, each with the need to talk, but not sure of what to say.

"You'll need to keep an eye on old Cronje. Food is being taken from the hotel larder without record. He isn't stealing but it messes up the costing of meals," said Claire.

"I really know very little about the hotel or how it's run. I'll need your help—and who is going to look after the farm?"

"The stores have decent managers but the hotel needs a lot of work. I will share what I know before I leave."

"You're sure about leaving?"

"I'm sorry, Tom. I don't want to leave you with a mess but I just can't stay."

"I understand."

"I'll come up once a month and help. Polo can help with the farming and hunting—he's been with you for quite a long time."

"I guess he could be trained to oversee things here. It's not that the farm provides any real income—the businesses bring in the money."

She looked out of the window and thought for a moment. "The corundum could provide a good income if you mine it."

I gave a short laugh. "I won't have time to oversee a mining operation as well."

"You won't have to do much, Tom. The government agency said they provide oversight—someone to direct the operations."

"For thirty percent of the profits," I argued.

"It's better than the mineral just lying there, going to waste."

I saw her point. My mind didn't want to accept the sudden absence of Willy-J's advice. "I'll figure something out."

Exhaustion overtook me and we decided to call it a day. I gave Claire a hug and headed for bed. She clung to me for a few seconds and I could feel her grief seep into my soul. Her body, soft and warm aroused a deep emotion within me but I quelled it with a sudden guilt. My brother's presence was everywhere. I could picture him with raised eyebrows—I imagined he could see my thoughts.

"I'll see you in the morning." My voice must have sounded a little strangulated; Claire gave me a strange look and nodded.

Sleep departed its usual rite of passage. My mind struggled with the idea of all the new the business responsibilities—thoughts fueled my insecurities and made me feel inadequate.

∞∞

EIGHT

Love is not blind but it leads to blindness.
—Auliq Ice.

The crow of old Pheko, the farmyard cockerel, heralded a new day as light filtered through the darkness of the night sky. I opened my eye-lids and squinted at the old clock on my dresser—five-thirty am.

The walk to the bathroom cleared my head and by the time ablutions came to an end the problem of the businesses reared its head again. Letsatsi busied herself in the kitchen with the wood-stove while I moved out onto the verandah to take in the sounds of the birdlife. The sun's warmth seeped into my bones and I observed the beautiful colors of the sky on the horizon. Although matters of the heart seemed bleak due to our loss, the bushveld's rituals remained unchanged. I could feel the heavy yoke of despair lift off my shoulders in response to the moment's nostalgia.

Claire appeared at the front door and breathed in the warm, freshness of the air. Summer would soon be upon us with its infestation of flies and mosquitoes; we needed to be careful of malaria, a common illness caused by the Tsetse fly.

"Good morning, Tom. It's magnificent, isn't it?"

"Yes—it's hard not to be able to enjoy the bushveld despite what has happened."

"Will loved this time of the morning. I'd often wake up and find him already out here, enjoying the sun."

The memory stung a little—Will and I enjoyed many conversations in this very spot. Turning inward, I felt a heaviness in my chest and limbs—the beauty of the scene before me disappeared and I could only stare at it with an emptiness.

"I'll be leaving for Pietersburg tomorrow so we need to spend the day visiting the businesses."

We can start as soon as breakfast is done," I agreed.

*

Mr. Greyling, chief surveyor for the Ministry of Mines, stuffed tobacco into his pipe and pointed to one of the rocks.

"As you can see Mr. Satherwaite, the corundum rocks are accessed from ground level and they run down, deep, into firmer soil. We'll need your workers to dig around the perimeter of the outcrop and clear away the topsoil."

He lit the pipe and the aroma wafted outward with each puff of smoke.

"I will provide you with an overseer who will make the journey from Pietersburg every Monday and leave again on the following Friday. He will provide for himself and stay in a tent onsite."

"How many workers do you think I need to employ?"

"At least twenty. The overseer will show them what to do—he is a qualified geologist and the government will cover his wages. You will need to cover the worker's wages, though. What you pay them is up to you."

The Mine operation didn't appear over complicated but I worried about the management details. The other businesses appeared to struggle without Willy-John's knowledgeable wisdom and our income, for each month, suffered a drop from four hundred Sterling to three-twenty per month. Old Cronje, at the hotel complained of midnight flits by customers and the occasional non-payment of bar tabs. Mrs. Joubert who ran the fabric store, whined about her wages and wanted me to look into the security angle—the disappearance, from time to time, of expensive cloth concerned her; Jan Venter at the butchery, suffered from a disease which kept him in bed from time to time and his young son Piet often ran the shop in his absence—meat disappeared every week and could not be accounted for; the farm implement and service also suffered certain losses and the proprietor couldn't pay his rental every month.

Willy-J would have all these problems resolved in a short space of time but I did not have the patience or the acumen for it. My forte lay in construction and supply of venison to the butchery. At least the Mine venture showed some promise for the future. How hard could it be to supervise a group of workers? Polo could act as overseer of the workforce under the guidance of Mr. Greyling's geologist.

Mr. Greyling's next words, however, caused me concern.

"Mining the rock is the most difficult part of the operation. You will need to purchase equipment to break up the crystal. Special drills and demolition hammers will be needed to make it a manageable process. I believe you will be able to find a steam-driven hammer in Pretoria—I suggest you make enquiries as soon as possible."

"Are these very expensive items?" I asked.

"I believe you should be able to lease them on a monthly basis. I have no idea as to the cost."

My plan for equipment had given no thought to monetary outlay. A firm in Louis Trichardt took care of all the business accounts—I realized I didn't even know the address of their office. Will always addressed these issues in the past and Claire, despite her promise to pay a visit once per month, remained an absentee partner—she understood more about finances than I. I could not help feel the disappointment at her silence. I sent money to the address in Pietersburg every month, but received zero response from her.

"I will see to it," I said.

After Mr. Greyling's departure I sat down at the kitchen table and drafted out a list of matters to attend to. The sound of horse-hooves attracted my attention— I walked out to the verandah to investigate but missed the anonymous rider who trotted the horse around to the stable. A pleasant surprise awaited me as I followed up to identify my visitor.

"Hello, my sweetheart." Olivia, my fiancé had come to visit. We had not seen each other for several days due to the distraction of the business problems.

"Good afternoon, my darling," I responded. "I guess you must have been missing me?"

"I thought you must have forgotten I existed," she complained.

"I apologize, my love—I've just finished with the agent from the Minister of Mines."

We embraced and kissed. The day after Claire left for Pietersburg Olivia and I made a decision to tie the knot. Tall and elegant, my fiancé wore her dark-brown hair in a ponytail and hypnotized every male with her beautiful emerald-colored eyes. Even without makeup, men often turned in the street to look at her. I realized I needed someone to share my life with, to make a home and raise a family and although she demonstrated issues, so did I.

Liv didn't know about the business problems and I refused to share them with her—compliments of my male pride. It surprised me when she came up with a good suggestion about the present state of affairs.

"I know you must have your hands full, Love—trying to jump into your brother's shoes so soon after his passing. My father has shown some interest in helping with the hotel and saloon."

"You mean, like a partnership?"

"No—he has offered to buy it from you and Claire. He feels you will need to concentrate on the corundum mining because it's where our fortunes will lie in the future."

I contemplated her words. The idea appeared to be sound but Claire needed to be on-board with it. I felt she might jump at an opportunity to sell off the businesses for cash.

"I will talk to Claire. It seems like a good idea to me. Are you staying over?"

She giggled. "My parents are not happy about it but we are engaged."

"It's too late for you to ride home now, anyway—so, let's make the best of it," I said.

"We need to wash before bed," said Olivia. She gave me a knowing smile.

"Once we're married I'll build a better bathroom and put in a bigger tub," I said.

I felt a little self-conscious about the amenities in the house. Willy-John's intension to remodel the bathroom with more modern items, from the stores in Pietersburg, never came to fruition and the whole aftermath of his death prevented me from any thoughts of new construction to the house. The old claw-foot, cast iron tub originally stood in the kitchen until Claire talked Willy-John into building a separate bathroom in 1908. Since that time nothing changed but now with Olivia I knew it would only be a matter of time before she complained about it. Her home on the farm near Louis Trichardt sported every modern adornment available.

"Is there hot water on the stove?"

"Don't worry, sweetheart. I'll bring it to you."

The rainwater tank, out at the back of the house, held about two thousand gallons for all our household needs. Letsatsi always left a pot of water on the old combustion stove outside the backdoor, for my nightly wash. In the bedroom, a washstand which contained a bowl, stood against one of the walls and a one half pitcher of water served as a sufficient ablution, before bed. A full bath of water took much more effort and as a rule we indulged the luxury only one evening per week. With Olive present, this would be the night for it.

I carried the large pot to the bathroom and poured the hot water into the old tub, then tempered it with cold from the rainwater tank. We both undressed and stepped into the warm water, to wash away the day's dust and grime, deeply conscious of each other's bodies. Despite Olivia's strong religious upbringing I knew she desired sexual contact and would not wait for the traditional consummation offered by legal marriage, a tradition strictly enforced by the elders of her church denomination.

I gestured with my eyes toward the bedroom and she smiled. We climbed out of the tub, toweled ourselves off and I extinguished the candles. With the house in darkness we stumbled naked, through to fall in a tangle of arms and legs, onto the bed. We made copious love and the day's tensions dissolved like the late-morning frost.

∞∞

NINE

The way to get started in business is to stop talking and start doing. *−Bill Todd.*

I believed my future marriage to Olivia would resolve many of the problems I faced, but guilt plagued my conscience−How could our marriage work if the real reason tended toward a union of convenience and physical attraction in opposition to true love? Olivia possessed a buoyant personality but she suffered severely from rejection and jealousy. Her father, a strict Boer farmer, made no bones about the fact he wanted a son, which his wife could not produce. Olivia and her three younger sisters testified to the problem.

Olivia decided to ride back to her parent's farm that morning. She did not want to sit around while I interviewed the twenty-five men chosen by Polo, for the Mine operation. Young men in their twenties posed a problem for consistent work ethic because all they wanted to do was drink, sleep and have sex with the young maidens in the village.

As Olivia mounted up on her horse, Letsatsi came from the hotel at a run with several bottles of

Brandy cradled in her arms—my order from the saloon. She appeared to be excited.

"Morena—the Medem, she is by the hotel."

"The Madame is at the hotel—which Madame?" I asked.

"The Medem, Claire. She cum from the Pietersbeg."

"Mrs. Claire?"

"Ee, Morena—wife for Morena Willy."

I looked at Olivia and I saw her jaw muscles tighten. We often quarreled about Claire's attitude. I told her Claire never stopped mourning Willy-J's sudden departure but Olivia wouldn't let up. The two never saw eye to eye. To make matters worse Olivia's jealous nature dictated her demeanor whenever we happened to be around other women. She felt they all held affection for me. She couldn't stand it when Claire wanted to talk to me alone about the businesses. After her departure to Pietersburg I sensed Olivia to be a much happier person.

"She probably wants to discuss the businesses. It will be a good time for me to talk about selling the hotel."

Olivia rolled her eyes in typical fashion. "Make sure she doesn't stay too long."

"I must discuss the mining operation with her—after all she is half owner of everything." I felt a little defensive and irritated by Olivia's attitude.

She shimmied up onto the horse and turned around to leave. I could see by the firm set of her jaw she felt threatened by Claire's sudden arrival. Without a backward glance she spurred the horse and rode off at a half-gallop.

I shrugged and told Letsatsi to relay a message to Polo—his men needed to be at the homestead by two pm for the job interviews. The height of the sun indicated enough time for me to make a quick visit to the hotel for a chat with my sister-in-law. In the stable my horse, Dreamer, waited to be saddled.

*

Claire sat in the lounge with a book in hand. At mealtimes the room became the dining facility, but in the afternoons, old Cronje made tea and coffee available to all who wanted to catch up on the latest news, tell jokes or enjoy some time together.

"What brings you back to Kweetsa at this time? I'm surprised to see you," I said.

"I thought it time for me to return and help you as promised."

I couldn't keep the anger out of my voice. "That was months ago. You haven't answered any of my letters or acknowledged the money I've sent."

Claire did the unexpected. She stood up from the chair and wrapped her arms around me. "I've missed you Thomas."

I gave her an involuntary kiss on the cheek and stepped back. "How long do you intend to stay?"

"As long as I feel is necessary. I've been speaking to Cronje and he feels things are not going as well as they should."

I became defensive. "I can handle the situation."

She looked at me with determination in her eyes. "Don't forget, I still own half of everything and I have a right to make sure things are being well managed."

My anger surfaced again. "Yes, you have a right, Claire—but don't forget you wanted to leave—you ran away, leaving me with the whole caboodle."

She softened her tone and took a step forward again, to place a hand on my arm. "Don't be angry, Thomas. We were always such good friends. I know with my help we can make a go of the businesses and I'm sorry it took me so long to get over my grief."

Her tone took the wind out of my sales and I felt guilty. "Olivia will be upset. I think she feels it should be her providing the helping hand."

"Olivia has less business sense than you do, Tom. I think she resents me because I'm your sister-in-law."

I knew Claire spoke the truth but my instincts told me trouble already brewed at Olivia's home regarding Claire's return.

"There is something we need to discuss regarding the hotel—Olivia's father wants to buy us out and run it. He says I'll have enough on my hands with the corundum mine."

Claire shook her head. "Not a good move at all, Thomas. We have no idea if the Mine will even be successful."

"But I can't keep my hand on everything here," I said.

She countered my outburst. "I'll make sure the hotel is well looked after. All old Cronje needs is some help. I thought of moving the piano back in here and playing it myself in the evenings."

I didn't know what further to say. The possibility of slow growth for the Mine operation presented a valid point. We still needed finances and the hotel, in conjunction with the butchery, still provided a reasonable income.

I sighed in resignation. I couldn't force Claire out and her plan seemed a good one. No reason other than Olivia's jealousy existed to force my hand—plus a desire to wash my hands of the businesses responsibilities.

"I will tell Olivia's father it's a no-go then but I know she won't take it lying down."

"I'm sorry if this will cause you some grief, Thomas, but I am still part-owner and she really has no say from a legal standpoint."

I glanced at the clock above the fireplace. I needed to get back to the house where Polo and his men waited to begin the interviews.

"Okay, it's settled then. You'll stay here, in the hotel and take charge of the other businesses while I get on with the farm and the Mine."

She smiled and stepped forward to give me another hug. I could smell the fragrance of her perfume as our cheeks touched and the softness of her skin felt like fine silk. Once again I chided myself for these thoughts. A widow at the age of thirty and as beautiful as Claire, would soon marry again.

The ride back to the house gave me an opportunity to regain my composure and when I arrived, a line of men squatted on their haunches in front of the verandah. Polo stepped forward with a large grin.

"Dem sum goot wekkers, Morena. Dis one, an' dis one—dey like me—goot wekkers."

I acknowledged his effort and sat down in my chair on the verandah to begin the interviews. The men came up the steps one at a time and squatted in front of me, some dressed in traditional blankets while others wore an assortment of clothes, which ranged between torn old pants and dirty shirts, to moth-eaten coats and tattered jackets—a real motley bunch.

I chose twenty men whom I thought might be best suited for the work and sent the rest back to the village. Polo pranced around with orders for everyone—he considered himself to be the "moetapele", person in charge.

I let him get on with it. The work would start in earnest, the next day.

They all moved off back to the village, with traditional songs on their lips, happy to be employed and it appeared everyone accepted the conditions of the arrangement. Later, after dinner I hauled out the brandy and poured myself a stiff drink in celebration. In truth, I felt glad to have Claire back again. A protective instinct, an emotion I could not quite understand, held me in its grip—her presence reassured me of Willy-J's legacy.

I did feel a deep affection for Olivia, though. She could be kind hearted at times and often looked out for my interests. My relationship with Claire, however, stemmed back many more years and contained one powerful factor—the attachment to the one person I loved more than anyone else—Willy-John.

I needed to make some enquiries about the Mine equipment. With Claire back in the harness a greater freedom dispelled my prior negativity. I could concentrate on the corundum venture and be singled minded about it.

My mind churned over the Mine operation requirements. The miners needed picks and shovels which I could get on tick from our Farm Implement and Service Center, in Kweetsa. An arrangement with the owner allowed Polo to collect the implements and get his workers onto the job. My intention of a trip to Pietersburg for the examination of the steam-hammer plus other necessary equipment, also occupied my thoughts and I lay awake long into the night.

The geological team surveyed another four areas to come up with more corundum-bearing rock and the prognosis for tonnage, measured in the thousands. Mr. Greyling felt confident of a potential market upswing in the near future and the consequent expansion of our workforce. I felt contentment an optimism—improvement to our quality of life appeared imminent. The new rail-terminus, close to our hotel location would bring greater traffic and with Claire in charge of the businesses, better management all round could be expected.

∞∞

TEN

It's an ill wind that blows no good. — John Heywood.

Three days later I returned from Pietersburg in the afternoon to find Olivia on the verandah. She came at a run to greet me while I disembarked from the saddle. I called for Letsatsi to stable Dreamer and took Olivia in my arms.

I felt good about the business contracted with the Mine equipment agent. A new steam jackhammer with drill would arrive from Pretoria by train within two weeks and the operation could start in earnest. I felt eager to impress my lady with the details.

"Hello my darling—how was your trip?" Olivia asked.

I could see she wanted to make amends for her attitude on the afternoon we heard the news of Claire's arrival.

"My trip turned out really great. I have arranged to lease some new equipment for the Mine and it will only take two weeks to arrive by train from Pretoria," I said.

She wrapped her arms around my neck and we kissed, both hungry for physical contact.

"Wonderful, my love. Have you decided about the hotel yet?"

The question came too soon for me but I didn't want to spoil the moment.

"We can talk about it later. Right now I just want to outspan and relax with a strong cup of coffee."

"Of course," she said. I could see the disappointment in her eyes.

We stepped up onto the verandah and sat down on the wooden love-seat, put together from the old timber remains of the homestead's roof construction. Letsatsi appeared with a tray of coffee and cookies, happy to see me.

"Polo him start dig todeh, Morena."

"Thank you, Letsatsi. I'm sure Polo will tell me all about it tomorrow. Please bring me my cigarettes."

She trundled off, back into the kitchen to retrieve my smokes. Olivia placed her head on my shoulder and we cuddled for a while, until Letsatsi returned with the cigarettes. Olivia didn't smoke, nor did she approve of the practice, but limited her remarks on the subject.

I recounted my three-day experience in Pietersburg and asked her what she had been up to.

"I have been doing a lot of sewing and embroidery work. My tapestry is also now complete."

"You've been a busy girl, then?"

She smiled and nuzzled into my neck. I knew she wanted to talk about the hotel so I decided to broach the subject of Claire's return to Kweetsa.

"Claire doesn't want to sell the hotel. She thinks she can make a good go of it."

I felt Olivia's body stiffen against mine for a brief moment.

"Is she going to stay?"

"She wants to help, Olivia, and she is entitled to Willy-John's half of the enterprise. I couldn't say no."

"I understand."

She sat up straight and looked out across the veld with a far-away look in her eyes. I could almost read her mind.

"When we get married you can move in here with me and we'll live our lives to suit ourselves," I added.

Olivia's silence spoke volumes and I could see she felt unhappy about Claire's intrusion. She nodded and rested her head on my shoulder again.

Letsatsi called from the kitchen to say the dinner awaited our attention and we moved into the dining room.

"I'll need to go hunting tomorrow. The butchery will be low on venison."

"Do you want me to do anything?" she asked.

"Perhaps you could look in on Polo and his workers. Make sure they have enough water to drink. You'll need to draw from the well."

"I will do as you ask, my husband to-be."

After the evening meal we settled back on the verandah to enjoy the cacophony of noise produced by the myriads of bush insects; the stars twinkled overhead and together, with a full moon, the veld produced an unforgettable, theatrical scene. After an hour we both felt the physical urge to retire to the bedroom.

Old Pheko woke me with the morning crow as the first light of dawn, filtered through into the room. Olivia's head rested on my chest and her one leg draped over my thighs. I reflected on the night before but after several minutes, nature called and I extracted myself with care so as not to wake her.

*

When I returned from the hunt at about midday a surprise visitor awaited me on the verandah—Mr. Potgieter, Olivia's father. He greeted me with a shake of the hand and I asked whether he would like something to drink but he declined.

"Where's Olivia?" I asked.

"I have sent her home because I want to talk to you man to man."

I stiffened at his words and the content of the dialog already started to form in my mind. I waited for him to launch his verbal assault but instead he remained calm.

"I understand that you two young people are in love, Thomas. I too was young once but we grew up under different rules. We were taught that a man and a woman, unmarried, should never be alone together, because temptation will let the devil in."

"I don't believe in the 'devil'. A fiery creature with a pitchfork and a tail doesn't appeal to me."

"It doesn't matter if you believe it or not— Olivia's mother and I do. She may be engaged to marry you but that does not make her your wife. Until she marries she remains under my authority because God wills it."

"I think your God and mine are very different," I said.

"What God do you serve, Thomas? The god who lives in a brandy bottle?"

I felt a sweat break out on my brow and I clenched my hands together but managed to remain silent.

"My family serves the God of the Bible and a father is responsible for his daughter. Can I ask you a question, Thomas?"

I raised my eyebrows.

"Did the two of you sleep together last night? Again I stared at him and said nothing.

"I take your silence as a 'yes'.

"Olivia is a big girl, Mr. Potgieter. She can make her own decisions."

He mumbled something in the Afrikaans language, which I took to be several swear words.

"It means little to us if she is of age or not. She is unmarried and still a part of my household. I will forbid her to visit here until the two of you are legally married in God's eyes."

"Good luck with that," I said. She is more like a wild mare and one I might add, you have never been able to tame."

My words must have stung because his eyes bulged in anger and for a moment I thought he might vomit. He levelled a murderous glare in my direction and stood to his feet, swayed back and forth for a few seconds and then stumped off down the stairs to his horse.

I remained seated. "I bid you goodnight, Mr. Potgieter. Please give my best your wife."

He galloped off at a furious pace without a backward glance. Letsatsi came out onto the verandah and handed me a note.

"Where did this come from," I asked.

"Other Morena he cum to talk dis morning."

A man came to see me this morning while I was out on the hunt?"

"Ee, Morena. He gif dis nott for you."

I opened the folded piece of paper and it read:

Dear Mr. Satherwaite,
Please meet me at the hotel tomorrow morning. I have a proposition for you.

Robert King.

∞∞

ELEVEN

Ambition is a good servant but a bad master.
– unknown

The next morning at eight-thirty I saddled Dreamer and rode to the hotel. A few patrons busied themselves with breakfast as I strolled in and old Cronje, on a walk between the kitchen and the lounge, shouted a greeting. Claire appeared from the passageway to the rooms and came over to the small reception area, where I waited.

She smiled, surprised to see me. "Hello Tom. How are you?"

"Good thanks—I believe there was someone wanting to see me?"

"Yes, a Mr. King, representing some company in England. He says he remembers you and Will from the war years."

The name rang a bell. Robert King commanded a regiment under General French and played a role in the relief of Kimberly. I remembered him from the battle of Modder River. Claire gave me an unexpected hug. "It's good to see you, Thomas."

I scuffed my boot against the foot-rail at the bottom of the reception counter and blushed.

"It's good to see you too, Claire—how are the businesses doing?"

"So, so—you know how it is—everyday delivers its challenges. I will get Mr. King for you."

I waited in the lounge and tried to relax on a large settee. A few minutes later Claire returned with Robert King in tow. He looked much like I remembered him; a large red-faced man with a mustache and long side-burns. He either spent a lot of time in the sun, or drank a lot of wine, perhaps both.

"Thomas Satherwaite. You haven't changed a bit from the day we first met at the Modder." King extended his hand to me as I stood to greet him.

"Mr. King," I said. "I see you haven't changed much either."

King first offered his condolences for the death of Willy-John before we sat down to exchange pleasantries and memories. After idle chatter about the war-days he broached the subject of his visit.

"Tom, I represent a large consortium in London who assist entrepreneurs with loans to start businesses. I see you and your sister-in-law have been quite successful lately."

I shifted in my seat. "Yes—although there have been challenges."

He stroked one of the long sideburns. "I understand you are embarking on a new venture?"

Claire must have shared our latest project with him. "Yes, a corundum Mine. We have discovered some large deposits of the mineral on the farm. I intend to mine it for domestic and export markets."

King leaned back on the settee. He possessed beady, eyes with black pupils and they locked onto mine with intensity.

"I believe my company, Corporate Business and Finance, could be of great help. You will need a lot of capital and equipment once the market catches on."

"I'm listening," I said.

We spoke for another half-hour before King finished off the presentation of his company's attributes and how successful partnerships with them worked to produce good profits. King convinced me the offer should transform our Mine venture into a successful enterprise and by the time he departed I felt set on the idea.

Claire returned from the kitchen and called out as I descended the hotel steps to the tether-rail where Dreamer waited.

"How did it go, Thomas?"

I didn't want to discuss the details with her at the time. After all, the corundum mine should be my responsibility. To have someone else involved, or assist with the decisions, didn't suit me at all.

"I need to consider some of things he offered but I can't discuss them now—I must get to the worksite."

I pulled on the rein to turn Dreamer's head and rode off at a trot. Claire stood hands on hips at the top of the stairs and I sensed her frustration. There existed no devious ambition to exclude her but I felt this should be handled by me. I needed to show everyone I could make good business decisions and develop a successful enterprise—if my actions meant a disappointment to Claire, so be it. I thought it expedient to check up on the work crew at the dig-site and steered Dreamer past the homestead.

On my arrival I found Polo strutting up and down the perimeter in anger.

"Dees bluddy wekkahs not listen to me, Morena"

"What's wrong, Polo?"

"I tellem dig by da rocks, trow sant to udderside. Dey trow sant bek in hole."

My face must have showed my amusement at his description of the antics because he broke into a sudden grin.

Cum—I show Morena how mush wek we finish."

He showed me a section on the other side of the rock formation. I could see an excavation of at least ten feet deep, which exposed the entire side of the rock formation. It appeared to go much deeper than we first thought. The black-grey streaks of crystal veins glistened in the sun—an indication of a greater mineral potential than first expected.

Satisfied at the progress I turned Dreamer around and galloped back along the dusty path, toward home. After lunch I could spend the rest of the afternoon in consideration of Robert King's suggestion of a partnership with the CBF Company and work on a game plan.

To have a company provide the financial outlay for equipment and take over some of the management responsibility suited me fine. My potential appointment as a director of a new company and profits shared out on a formula acceptable to both parties, excited me. It sounded idyllic and I doubted a better deal for the Mine operation existed.

King promised to return in two weeks, on his way back from Beit Bridge to Pretoria, with the prospect of further discussion and to hear what I thought of the whole idea. I felt sure Willy-J would have approved. A strong and well-situated company on my side, to provide the bulk of finances and expertise, meant less pressure on me.

After lunch I settled down on the verandah and listened to the sounds of the bushveld. The Piet-my-vrous called to each other and the occasional cry of a "Go-away" bird floated on the air. I wasn't sure if God existed but when my ear tuned into the bushveld's vibrant life I got a distinct impression the creator lived in his creation and spoke through it.

A horse-rider appeared in the distance, on the move toward the house at a fast trot. I strained my eyes and could make out a woman in the saddle—Olivia. I felt a sudden need to share my future with this lady. She may have issues but I knew she loved me and wanted to be at my side as much as possible. The fact she often rode on horseback for three hours from Trichardt, despite the dangers, spoke volumes to me.

I knew her family did not appreciate her riding alone, and as borne out by her father's recent visit, much of the problem lay in the 'immoral' impression' our relationship presented to others. To stay the night with a man, outside the union of church marriage, constituted a violation of religious laws propagated by the Bible and held with strict implementation, by the church people.

It frustrated them greatly. A religious family, brought up on strict Calvinist values, the Potgieters believed in marriage before sex. The younger generation, of course entertained different ideas.

The horse trotted up to the house and I came down the stairs to grab the reins.

"Hello my love. So glad you could come today," I said.

"I wanted to be with you, Thomas. Wild horses couldn't keep me away."

"Not even your dad by the looks of it."

"I'm so sorry, sweetheart. I didn't know he would spy on us. I hope he didn't upset you."

"He only wants to protect you, darling. I kept my cool throughout his little morality speech but he didn't leave a happy man."

I helped her dismount and she collapsed into my arms, happy as a lark. We swirled around a few times with her feet off the ground and she squealed in delight. Hormones took over and I carried her to the bedroom much to the chagrin of Letsatsi, whom I sensed did not like Olivia much.

I closed the door and we proceeded to divest each other of clothes before falling like two sacks of grain onto the bed in a flurry of limbs. With the wedding a week away we threw all caution to the wind—I never thought about children in the equation but it is what young people in love do. The sooner the better—I stood on the verge of a vast fortune and family life suited me—no time like the present to settle down.

After supper we moved out onto the verandah to sit on the bench and I lit up a cigarette. With Letsatsi adjourned to the village the remains of the evening belonged to Olivia and I—a good time for me to share the latest news.

"I had a visitor come to the house while I was on the hunt yesterday. A guy Willy-J and I knew during the war. He left a note for me."

Olivia registered a sudden memory. "It must have been the man whom I passed on the road after my father sent me home."

"Your father must have been here when the fellow arrived but he never said a word to me about it."

"Maybe he was too angry."

Olivia rested her head on my shoulder and I kissed her on the forehead. "This man works for a company in England who wants to help me with the mining operation. They're offering to put up all the finances and help with management."

"She sat up and looked at me. "In exchange for what?"

"A formal contract, signed by both parties makes me the director of a new company. Shares can be floated on the stock exchange one day resulting in enormous profits for us. This type of promotion is not anything I could ever manage by myself."

"It sounds like a logical thing to do," said Olivia.

"I'm seriously thinking of taking them up on it."

"We'll be rich—richer than my parents." I could see Olivia warm to the idea.

"I'll need to see a lawyer and ask him some questions. I think there is a law firm in Pietersburg."

"Doesn't this company have lawyers? Why pay for something they will provide?"

This made sense but I never gave thought to the hidden agendas lawyers entertain in order to fleece their clients.

We decided to hit the sack and call it a night.

The next morning I woke with a start. Old Pheko's continued cocka-doodle-doos and the fowl's frightened cackles indicated an out of the ordinary situation in the backyard. The old cockerel sounded flustered and annoyed at the same time so I slipped out of bed and went to the window. I couldn't see the cause of the fowl's indignation so I pulled on my dressing gown and walked to the kitchen door. Outside, in the semi-light, I could make out the hens all a-flutter, up in the air one second and down on the ground the next.

On closer inspection a dead hen in the sand, outside the coop, caught my attention. The cause might be one of two problems; a jackal or a snake. A snake might be after the eggs and a jackal, the hens. I went back inside to get the flashlight and returned. When I walked toward the hen coop I saw a huge snake slither out of the entrance and make its way to the side fence. The Mauser is not the right weapon for such a problem, I needed the shotgun. If I went back inside to get it the snake would be gone before I returned. I hated to kill these animals but if I didn't the hotel would end up short of eggs and chickens for the menu. I spied a garden spade on the ground, beside the implement shed, a handy weapon for the intended purpose. I picked it up and struck at the body of the serpent without realization of the danger my action might incur, even if the blade hit its mark—the reason for this consideration—a black mamba is not an ordinary snake.

∞∞

TWELVE

The honey is sweet but the bee has a sting. —
Ben Franklin.

Mambas are the most dangerous and ven-
omous of snakes in all Africa. Had I known this to
be the species in the yard I would have allowed it
to go its way. The mamba is able to lift its head to a
height of three, or four feet, in the long grass when
confronted, or near its nest. I am told, the most
magnificent sight to see is one flee before a veld
fire. Eight years of bush experience negated any
experience of these snakes in our area. Their general choice of habitat is more east of Kweetsa and I
thought the serpent in the yard to be a more harm-
less species.

I stepped backward after the delivery of the
blow to the mamba's body. Due to the speed of the
snake's movement the spade did not sever its back
but glanced off the tough hide with minimal injury. The snake turned in retaliation.

I think old Pheko might have saved my life because at the moment the snake struck backwards
at me the cockerel fluttered across the strike zone.
I'm not sure if the fangs caught the feathers of his
wing or missed but he still fluttered around with
concern after the fact. The snake took off toward

the fence and disappeared into the morning gloom. The fowls fell into near hysteria. It took about ten minutes for them to settle down again. I removed the dead hen. The mamba—at least ten feet in length and two or three inches thick at the center of its body must have been after a chicken. They feed on birds and small rodents.

By this time, after all the noise Olivia came to the kitchen door, curious to see the cause of the tumult. I told her about the incident and she chided me on the need to have known better. One bite and I would have joined Willy-J in a matter of about twenty minutes—at the time, no anti-venom existed for the bite.

After breakfast we decided to saddle up and take a ride down to the hotel. On arrival we tethered the horses to the rail outside the reception and walked up the stairs, through the open doors into the foyer.

Claire happened to be at the desk behind the counter. She looked up. "What brings you folk to the hotel so early?"

"Oh, we thought it good to see how things are going," said Olivia.

I saw Claire's body stiffen as she glared at my fiance'.

I chose the impasse to intervene. "Just passing through—thought I might ask if the butchery needs any venison."

Claire's face gave away her thoughts; I knew I would hear about it later. Olivia is a good woman but she, all too often, speaks what's on her mind without thought of the implications.

"Did you hear Thomas is going to sign up with an English company?" said Olivia.

Claire looked at her through narrowed eyelids. "No, actually, I didn't—Tom was going to share something with me but he needed to get out to the worksite."

I jumped in to pour oil on troubled waters. "I didn't have the time yesterday but I wanted to tell you more about it this morning," I lied.

Claire turned her eyes on me. "Do tell, Thomas—after all, I am a partner in the Mine venture as well."

I detected the obvious sarcasm and could have cursed Olivia for her thoughtlessness.

My explanation of King's offer, followed. "I haven't decided one hundred percent to go with King's plan yet but it looks all very positive to me," I said.

Claire listened to all my reasons before she voiced her own reservation.

"I don't trust this Robert King. He seems too smooth for my liking. I think you should see a lawyer, Thomas—before we enter into any agreements with him or his company."

"I intend to. I think his above board—he's a British officer, or was one during the war—fought at Modder River and rescued old Cecil Rhodes from disaster at Kimberly."

"I don't give a hoot about the fact he might have been an officer several years ago—people change. I still don't like it," she countered.

Olivia came to my rescue. "I believe Tom can think for himself. He knows what he wants to do and I think it's a wonderful idea Mr. King has come up with."

Claire made a face and looked away. I felt awkward about the whole conversation and regretted the visit. I should have waited for a better opportunity.

"Well, it's time for us to go." I rose to my feet and helped Olivia up. "I will talk to you about the matter at another time and we can make a decision on it."

Olivia and I walked out of the hotel escorted by a furious Claire. As we mounted up to leave, Claire made one more point.

"Remember what Will used to say, Thomas. "Be careful what you wish for—"

I nodded and turned Dreamer's head for home.

*

The wedding day drew closer with one personal dilemma for me—Willy-J should have been my best man. After some thought I decided to ask

Polo. I thought about Olivia's reaction to a black man's presence at the wedding. Her parents would have a fit but it didn't worry me. Despite all their discriminatory overtones the Potgieters came across as good people. I understood the history of white and black in South Africa but it's not an experience I could relate to. I found it preposterous for anyone to look down on someone else because of their skin's color. It never occurred to me there might be a lot more to this history than I understood.

The night before the wedding I asked Polo over to the farmhouse for a drink of brandy. He came but I could see he felt very self-conscious. After a few drinks, however, he loosened up and became enamored with the idea of a best man role. I needed to find a suit to fit him—I did not want him to arrive in his traditional garb and send the Potgieters into a religious Armageddon. To have a black man in the church already created a huge challenge for the Afrikaans dominated community. Olivia asked me a week or so earlier as to whom the best man might be—I told her not to worry.

The fabric store carried a limited range of men's clothes and I made a deal with the manager about a suit I thought should fit Polo. Letsatsi picked it up from the store for me.

I suggested Polo try the suit on but our inebriated minds could not quite get it done in an orderly fashion—his impromptu dress rehearsal would have brought the comedy critics to their knees with laughter. He, of course, had never worn a suit and tie in his entire life. The pants turned out to be a bit baggy, but to find a perfect fit in the store, defied any sense of reality. The sleeves covered his hands with finger-tips exposed. The shirt, buttoned up to the collar, left a gap between his Adam's apple and the top button which I could fit my hand into. We both ended up on the ground in laughter, unable to contain our mirth. Polo staggered off to the village at ten-thirty, with his traditional sticks on hand in case of attacks by wild animals and I, still dressed in hunting clothes, fell onto my bed in a drunken stupor.

The next morning, the day of the wedding, I awoke to Pheko's usual side-show—my head felt like a piece of concrete and I dozed off again. At eight-thirty Letsatsi, woke me from a deep, inebriated sleep, fearful of the time constraint. Polo and I might miss the ceremony. The church service in Louis Trichardt, due to start at two pm sharp, still required a good three hours travel on horseback.

She offered me breakfast which I refused and ran off to the john for a quick puke session—I discovered, one tot of brandy, taken on an occasional evening, did not give me the ability to imbibe as I wished.

Polo arrived at ten. I could see he also suffered the consequences of over indulgence. His eyes, almost blood-red around the pupils, looked like trails in the veld and for a black man, he appeared pale. The two of us took one look at each other and tried to stifle the mirth. This resulted in another visit to the john. Letsatsi couldn't understand why we both wobbled around on unsteady legs but I produced two empty brandy bottles which caused her eyes to fly wide open in dismay. There appeared to be one remedy—a large bowl appeared on the verandah floor, which she filled with cold water. Polo suffered the indignation first as she dunked his head into the bowl and held it there. I exploded with laughter and fell over onto my back. Tears rolled down my cheeks, accompanied by expressive pig-like snorts but soon my turn came. Letsatsi dunked me as well. She held my head down until my lungs wanted to explode. Polo took his turn of mirth and a few moments later the two of us lay on our backs in tears and laughter. Letsatsi didn't find it funny and made indignant sounds of exasperation at our immaturity.

Under the circumstance we got dressed with as much speed possible but our attempts to leave on time, looked dismal.

∞∞

THIRTEEN

Marriage is more than finding the right person. It's being the right person. —unknown.

By eleven, Polo and I sobered up enough to drag ourselves onto the horses for the trip to Louis Trichardt. I told Letsatsi where to find the ring in my dresser. She stuffed it into Polo's suit pocket and warned him not to lose it. I doubt whether either of us remembered the trip but three hours later we arrived at the Louis Trichardt Reformed Church, where several families waited at the front entrance. I couldn't help but laugh at Polo, his suit all dusty and oversized and his face a picture of forced sobriety.

We tethered the horses at the rail behind the church and made our way to the main entrance. I shall never forget the scene. The Minister stood at the door to greet guests along with Mrs. Potgieter and Olivia's two sisters. Claire, as pretty as a picture in a blue dress and smart white hat, stood to one side. The sight of her brought back a memory of the days when she, Willy-J, and I, used to tease each other and have fun at functions. Often, after a day's outing, we would race each other home to the farm and chat on the verandah for hours.

The Minister stared at the two of us as we approached the entrance but when he saw Polo, his eyes widened in horror. Trouble stalked my every step toward the church door; Polo appeared to be the lone, black guest.

The Minister stopped us before we could enter. He struggled to keep his composure.

"Who is this fellow?" he asked. I detected the indignation in his voice and a frightened Polo froze on the spot. I doubt if it ever entered his mind Olivia and I would be married in an Afrikaans church.

"This is my best man, Polo." I answered.

"I'm afraid there must be some mistake, Thomas," returned the Minister. "Blacks are not allowed in the church."

I tried to remain calm. "But this is a house of God—surely anyone is welcome?"

"This fellow is a heathen and I cannot allow him to enter. I'm sorry but you should have known."

Olivia's mother closed her eyes and looked as though she might faint. I doubted a silent prayer offered on my behalf, rather the summons for a bolt of lightning, to end my life.

She turned to the Minister and uttered the most egregious remarks in the Afrikaans language. Olivia's two sisters stared in astonishment at their mother's reaction as did the other guests. I felt rage within me at the hypocriticalness of the situation. The sudden need to vent in non-appropriate and passionate terms, overcame me. Claire, however, stepped to my side and grabbed my arm. She turned me around with a "follow me." Polo joined us with nervous glances over his shoulder as we walked around to the back of the church.

"Thomas—what on Earth were you thinking? You know these people belong to a very strict Afrikaner denomination. They think the blacks don't have souls and you are not going to change it —certainly not by disregarding their beliefs like this."

"I didn't think they would mind on such a special occasion," I said.

"Thomas, no matter what we think about the matter this is their church and their belief. If you wanted to marry Olivia under a different denomination you should have said so."

I sunk my face into my hands. I didn't want to believe people could be so rigid.

"I guess I've really blown it this time," I murmured.

Claire pulled me to her and slipped an arm around my waist. "We can still rescue the situation, Tom. Just tell Polo to give you the ring and to stay outside with the horses. I will come into the church with you."

I contemplated her gesture. "Thanks, Claire—I see your point but perhaps I should go into the church alone. Olivia will be upset if you and I come in together."

She made a face. "You are probably right. There has been enough trouble for one day—you go in alone."

I spoke to Polo and related my sincere apology at his exclusion. I believe to this day, he felt a great sense of relief. He handed me the ring, which I placed into the pocket of my waistcoat and sauntered off to sit down near the horses.

"No wurry, Morena—no problem."

I sensed release on both our parts but underneath, seethed at the ignorance of the religious establishment and vowed it would be the last time I ever entered a church. Claire accompanied me back to the entrance, where the Minister eyed me with a stony glare. We walked past him without comment and I took my place in the front pew to await the arrival of the bride.

Olivia arrived in a carriage drawn by a white horse and all my pent-up tension departed as I gazed at her in awe. Her wedding gown, draped on the floor behind and carried by four young girls in floral dresses, exemplified the aspect of spiritual beauty. Mr. Potgieter walked in beside her, dressed in a black suit followed by the two sisters, each with a flower bouquet. Olivia looked beautiful and my heart lurched as she came up alongside me. The rest of the ceremony went off without a hitch but I felt a deep disquiet about poor old Polo, outside at the back of the church. It took an effort on my part to push it from my mind and concentrate on the vows.

The Minister faked his smile and I detected his concealed anger at my fatal offense in the near desecration of his precious house of worship. He repeated some sentences in English for my benefit so I could respond to the vows, but it all went over my head. My eyes stayed glued to Olivia's. The end result of the ceremony is what mattered the most—I didn't care about the language—I felt sure God, if he indeed existed, understood.

After the reception my bride and I climbed into the carriage, a gift to us from the parents, and returned to Kweetsa for our first night as a married couple. Polo followed on his own horse with Dreamer in tow. Olivia knew little about the catastrophic best-man issue, until I told her.

Contrary to my assumptions about her attitude toward black people she laughed and apologized for her parent's rigidity and stressed she never allowed them to tar her with the same brush. I think she desired to escape the church as much as I did.

*

A week later an important message arrived via one of the train passengers, who stayed over for one night at the hotel—a letter from Robert King in confirmation of his visit.

The wedding and its aftermath disrupted all thought of the potential offer regarding the Mine operation but now we could get back on track again. I intended to spend several days at the dig-site and another two on the hunt but changed my plans in anticipation of King's visit. My hope of a decision about the farm's future now loomed with great expectation for our future but a measure of anxiety surrounded my usual fatalistic mindset.

Olivia felt inclined to accept the offer. "It will be a great help for you, my darling," she said. "Just think of the trouble we save ourselves and there will be no need for you to see a lawyer—it will only cost us unnecessary money."

I recalled Claire's counsel on this same matter. "I'm not so sure, honey."

"Oh come on, Thomas. What can go wrong?"

I couldn't visualize what might go wrong. Perhaps Willy-J might not have been so quick to accept King's proposal but my brother no longer featured in the equation. With Claire's hands filled with the problems generated by the businesses I felt any decisions with regard to the farm's future, should lie on my shoulders. It didn't seem fair to burden her with the details of the proposal.

"I'll talk further to King about any liabilities which might affect the business. He will be here on Saturday."

"Wonderful, darling—now give me a kiss."

Olivia always brought our conversations back to physical touch. She did not have a great propensity for business matters, perhaps because her father never shared the finances of his farm operation with her. She spent most of her days with her mother, involved in tapestry work and embroidery of clothes. The men took total charge of their families in the Afrikaans culture and ruled with an iron hand. A woman's place involved the cleanliness of the house and the daily comfort of their men. I never thought this to be an ideal practice. To me, women possessed the most wonderful gifts and I hoped to share as much of the blood, sweat and tears with my new bride—I felt Olivia would be up to it.

*

Robert King arrived on the afternoon train from Beit Bridge and requested a little time to refresh himself before our chat. I asked Claire if she'd like to sit with us but old Cronje came down with a sudden cold and left her to oversee the bar and the kitchen.

"You can fill me in later with the details, Thomas," she said.

I took this as a vote of confidence in my ability to assess the details of the partnership and future prospects of the Mine.

We moved into the lounge to sit in front of the fireplace and wait for King to make an appearance. Olivia grabbed my hand and we cuddled for a short while. The man made his appearance some fifteen minutes later. He took Olivia's hand and kissed the delicate white knuckles in pompous emulation of an ambassador. I extended my hand which he shook with vigorous energy.

"So good to see you two again—I believe congratulations are in order."

Olivia smiled. Her beautiful, straight white teeth glinted in the overhead light.

"We are also very glad to see you again, Mr. King—Mr. and Mrs. Satherwaite now at your service."

We sat down again and exchanged small talk. A kitchen attendant brought in coffee and poured each of us a cup while King settled himself into the chair to talk about the potential of the partnership.

"If you come in with us, Thomas, you will receive a director's remuneration of at least one thousand pounds sterling per annum. I can't say exactly how much it will be because many assessments will still have to be made on the market itself."

Olivia's eyes lit up. "A thousand Pounds is a very good income, Mr. King."

"Please call me Robert. I will see to it—you, as a couple, will profit magnificently through all this.

The company I work for is very good to its employees and partners."

In the end both Olivia and I expressed our appreciation of the company's ability to deliver its promised benefits and I felt at peace with the whole deal. CBF required me to sign a contract with them—a 'document of great promise' as he called it, the dictates to which both parties are bound.

"I will have to get my sister-in-law to sign with me. She owns my late brother's share of the farm."

"I'll leave the document for you to scrutinize and your sister-in-law can sign it when she's ready," he said.

I agreed and we shook hands. He beamed at us and called for drinks from the saloon to celebrate the partnership. Olivia and I came up with the name "Black Rock Corundum," and I filled it in on the articles of association which King left with me. He said their company lawyers did all the documentation for the new enterprises. I decided not to include Claire in the directorship of the new company—a percentage of the profits belonged to her because of Willy-John's ownership of the farm's mineral rights. Black Rock Corundum belonged to Olivia and I.

We drank a hearty toast to our new union and left King to get his rest as the next train to Pretoria departed at six in the morning.

We found Claire at the desk in the reception. She held up a written notice in one hand. "I have given the matter of Mr. King's offer a lot of thought. As you know I'm not happy with the deal but I do not want to stand in your way, Tom."

I leaned against the counter. "What are you proposing?"

"I want to protect the businesses Will worked so hard to build while he lived. The Corundum Mine is a new venture which didn't materialize until after his death—I propose we split the farming operation along with the mine, from the hotel and other businesses."

"I'm listening," I said. Olivia rolled her eyes.

Claire continued with her suggestion. "The corundum mine, if viable appears to be worth a lot of money—much more than the businesses. I propose you take over the farm and the Mine—I will take over the hotel and its related businesses here in the village. You run with Mr. King's idea and make your fortune. I will continue and make do with the Hotel."

I thought over the implications as best I could. I looked at Olivia who smiled and nodded her agreement with the plan. To be rid of Claire pleased her no end.

Claire added another suggestion. "You can continue to supply the butchery with beef and venison plus the hotel with vegetables and eggs. I will pay you for this so you will have a regular income to live while the Mine gets up and running."

This sounded like a good idea to me. "I like it," I said. "This way you are protected if anything goes wrong and only the farm will be involved with King's plan. If things go south you still have the businesses."

Olivia couldn't resist a final word. "I think it's a great idea—we will be responsible for our own decisions. We have already made plans to form a company called Black Rock Corundum."

Olivia's admission embarrassed me and I didn't want Claire to think we felt her opinion to be of no consequence. . "I intended to tell you about it. King's lawyer will do all the paperwork," I said.

Claire gave a thin smile. "Well there you are— you both have been making plans without me so it only goes to show we'll both be better off running our own enterprises."

I blushed but the statement went over Olivia's head and she nodded her agreement.

"I'll have the lawyer in Trichardt draw up the agreement," said Claire. I could see by her attitude she wanted no further talk on the matter.

Olivia and I left for the farm. Mixed emotions plagued me but the more I thought about the deal the clearer I saw the future. As it turned out later Claire's foresight saved her a whole bunch of trouble. ∞∞

FOURTEEN

The only real mistake is the one from which we learn nothing. —*J. Powell.*

The leased equipment, to extract the corundum, performed the task with less efficiency than Mr. Greyling led me to believe. Chisels broke against the hard crystal with regularity and the small portable steam turbine for the hammer also gave its fair share of trouble.

The Chamber of Mine's geologist, Bertie Bakstrom, a native of Sweden and recent immigrant to South Africa, did his best to fix the equipment as it broke but in the end I decided to purchase a whole pallet of chisels. This cost a small fortune and I decided to use my new acquisition of a credit facility, set up by the bank in Pietersburg. Bertie, still new in the field, spent many a weekend at work on broken equipment. I feared for his marriage.

"This equipment will be the death of me," he often said to which I made my standard reply —"you don't have to fix everything, Bert. I will employ someone to do it."

His stock answer to my solution: "I know, Thomas, but I want this to be a success."

One day he got mad with the whole affair, jumped onto his horse and never returned. I tried to contact Mr. Greyling to let him know but my notices never drew a response. Polo kept the operation alive, thanks to Bertie who treated him like an apprentice—at least Polo would never quit on me.

I read through my contract with CBF again and again to find any clause of a time limit for the promised financial input. To my chagrin no such provision could be found. I understood from Robert King, their company's deposit of a cheque into a director's bank account every month constituted normal practice, but six months down the road, the CBF Company made no deposits of any kind. To keep the operation current I dipped into my own meagre savings and used the line of credit from my bank to its maximum. With it now depleted, I could no longer finance further operation.

Olivia remained positive. "Don't worry, Thomas. I'm sure Mr. King will come up with an answer."

"I think Mr. bloody King is taking us for a ride," I said.

Olivia made comments of frustration whenever I complained about the finances. "Perhaps you should have been more aware, Thomas. What are we going to do?"

My ilk rose at the suggestion of my impropriety.

"How do you think I feel, Olivia? Do you think I can see the future?"

She burst into tears and confessed certain comments, in regard to my lack of business acumen, made by her parents on her last visit home.

"Father says you don't have a business bone in your body. He suggested I have married a dumb Englishman."

I retaliated. "Your parents have never liked me. They are just stupid, dumb, thick Afrikaners who are all twisted up in their religion."

She stormed off into the bedroom and slammed the door. I let her be and walked outside onto the verandah to cool down. The legal implications of my contract concerned me to the point of distraction. Old Cronje made mention one evening in regard to the young lawyer who did the agreement between Claire and I. His new practice, recently started in Trichardt, showed great promise—maybe I could approach him for some advice about the CBF contract. It may be expedient for me to make a trip, come morning, to see this clever young fellow.

Later I entered our bedroom to undress for bed. Olivia lay with her back toward me and I, in my pride, turned my back on her. After several restless hours we both fell asleep—our first big argument since the wedding.

The next morning neither of us spoke to the other and I saddled Dreamer for a ride to Louis

Trichardt. With the contract tucked into the saddlebag Dreamer and I departed the farm at a gallop, followed by a trail of dust. The three-hour ride passed without incident and I arrived in the small town, to search for the lawyer's home.

I soon found my way to Van Tonder Street, and knocked on the front door of the home. Young Pieter Vermeulen opened on the third knock and invited me in. I told him about my need.

"Let's have a look at this contract," he said.

I handed the papers over and shared the details about the farm, the corundum business and Robert King's offer. Vermeulen scrutinized the contract while I waited. After ten minutes he looked up with a sympathetic frown. "I think you might have been taken in with the wording here, Mr. Satherwaite."

I felt the ice-cold grip of legal torture take hold of my mind. "How do you mean," I asked.

"The contract stipulates you must keep the mining operation going until such time as this Company, CBF, supplies the finances to run it but they have not committed to a date of such financing."

"But how can this be?"

"I have seen this before, Mr. Satherwaite. A company keeps the owner of a property waiting for promised finances, forcing the property owner to keep an operation going with his own personal capital. The owner eventually is bankrupted and the company steps in to take the property over as a part of the owners default."

I went cold all over and started to shake. Concerned for my well-being Vermeulen called his mother who brought me a cup of strong tea. I never in all my deliberations thought there might be a problem. Willy-J would have seen through the bogus contract in a heartbeat.

When I found my voice again I cursed Robert King and his trickery. "Is there any way I can get out of this contract?"

"I'm afraid not Mr. Satherwaite. You have signed off on all the conditions. The company will come up with an ironclad reason to not make the finance payments at this stage. You should have been more vigilant my friend. If you had brought it to me before signing I could have served you better."

My brain could not compute the enormity of my mistake—now the farm might be lost.

"What about the mineral rights of the lease? They can't take that away—it belongs to the government," I cried.

"The lease is in your name, Mr. Satherwaite and the company will simply tell the government you have defaulted on the mining agreement and CBF will take over the lease. The contract posits the mineral rights to be collateral for the delivery of the required tonnage to London. "

"I know the contract stipulates I have to deliver the tonnage—and we have so far. We have shipped four-hundred tons, now sitting at the London docks waiting for removal to their warehouse, but so far no one has bothered to pick the shipment up."

"Which means you are liable for the accumulated fees. They have cleverly worded this contract, Mr. Satherwaite. You will lose the farm plus the mineral rights unless you come up with the money to keep the enterprise running and keep the stated delivery schedule going. You will have to keep paying until such time they are ready to provide bridge financing."

"I have already run out of money and the bank won't allow me any more funds."

"I'm sorry I can't be of any help to you Sir. Consider this as a free consultation. You will have enough cost as it is, in bearing these consequences."

I thanked him and left. I don't recall the ride back to Kweetsa. The contempt I felt for Robert King fogged my mind to such an extent I determined, if I ever got my hands on him, he'd pay for his trickery.

∞∞

FIFTEEN

There's no love without pain. — Irving Stone.

"Where is Mrs. Olivia?"

"She go for walk, Morena," said letsatsi.

I always cautioned Olivia to take one of the rifles whenever out for a stroll. Dangerous predators still roamed the veld in our area and the possibilities of attacks still existed. I checked the rifle-rack above the fireplace in the lounge—all the guns hung on their respective holders. I needed to find Olivia as soon as possible. We parted earlier without a word to each other and the previous evening's argument still weighed on my mind.

With Mauser in hand I walked off into the veld, along the path toward the dig-site—it seemed the most logical direction for her to go. On arrival at the corundum rocks I spoke to Polo.

"Have you seen Mrs. Olivia?"

"Tjhee, Morena. No Missus Olif."

The safest places to take a walk might not even have occurred to Olivia and a panic set in—where might she have gone? When angry, she gave little consideration for safety and at times committed senseless acts. Mrs. Potgieter once told the story of Olivia, who denied certain privileges by her father for some transgression, walked off onto their farm one evening without any consideration of the family's concerns for her safety. Her father searched for hours until the family dog discovered her amongst the cattle in the kraal. He beat her with a leather strap but the intervention of her mother saved the young girl from serious injury. Mrs. Potgieter threatened to shoot her husband with a shotgun unless he relented. Brought to his senses by his wife's action he never placed a hand on any of the children again. Liv often sulked if she didn't get her own way but otherwise, she treated everyone with respect and dignity.

The afternoon wore on while I made a search of certain areas, but after two hours no sign of Olivia could be found. The path from the dig site meandered through a patch of Jackleberries which obscured the house from view. On eventual arrival at the verandah steps I saw her, in the chair next to mine, drinking coffee. Relief flooded my anxious mind and I hastened toward the steps with a smile on my face. The dogs lifted their heads to gaze at me with minimal interest and went straight back to sleep.

"I've been searching all over for you."

She looked down at the cup in her hands and her eyes made no contact with mine.

"You should always take one of the rifles with you if go out for a walk."

She looked up at me, and her eyes brimmed with tears.

"I didn't really go anywhere, Thomas—I was sitting out of sight, under the old Mopane tree. I didn't want to talk to you after the things you said about my family."

The frustration I felt at her lack of concern for my anxiety and her safety disappeared under an avalanche of sudden guilt. I did say some mean words and it needed to be put right.

"Liv, I'm sorry—but you must understand how angry the situation at the church made me and now this situation with the farm. I didn't mean those things—I apologize."

There would be no way out of this self-dug hole but to eat humble pie. For the moment, the world conspired to force me to my knees and expose my many failures. I seldom immerse myself in self-pity but the present situation offered an opportunity to indulge it.

Olivia dabbed at her eyes with a handkerchief and looked out over the veld. "I felt very hurt by your remarks, Thomas."

"All I can do is say I'm sorry, my sweetheart—I didn't mean to hurt you."

She managed a wan smile. "I forgive you." She dabbed again at the tear-filled eyes and I knelt next to the chair and took her head in my hands. She flung her arms around my neck and kissed me full on the mouth.

"Please let's never fight any more," she said. I looked into her emerald eyes and saw the Olivia I married—the girl who loved me and despite her issues, cared about what happened to me.

"Did you go to see the lawyer?" she asked.

I broke the bad news of our plight and the possible loss of the farm with its mineral rights. With a quiver in my voice the story of Robert King's black heart and my total miss-judgement of his character, flowed like a waterfall from my lips.

Olivia, stunned into silence, held both my hands in hers.

"What do you mean we could lose the farm?"

I shared the details of the lawyer's assessment. "It's all my fault. Claire warned me there might be dangers involved but I refused to listen."

"I'm sorry, Thomas—I egged you on to do the deal. I must also carry some of the blame."

"But, I'm supposed to be your protector, Olivia. I made the final decision."

She took my face in her hands and kissed my lips. "Don't worry, my darling—we'll see this through together."

"We already owe the bank for all the money spent on the shipped corundum. I believe there's a sudden downswing in its demand, due to the possibilities of a war between Britain and Germany. Our shipment is sitting on a wharf in London, gathering dust and storage fees. King's Company refuses to remove it to a warehouse—if only Willy-John still lived—none of this would have happened."

"How much longer will this go on for—before they decide to foreclose?"

"I don't really know. They'll have taken notice our operation, together with deliveries, has stopped," I said.

Olivia gave me a troubled look. "You have a contract to supply venison and vegetables to the hotel; if we lose the farm we will have no income."

"I'm sure Claire will be able to find a new supplier but I should let her know. I'll have to eat humble pie with her—her instincts about King were correct."

"When will you talk to her?"

"Tomorrow."

After dinner we sat on the verandah and sipped at our coffee while the two dogs slept next to our chairs, oblivious of all the troubles we faced. I finished my cigarette and we decided to call it a night.

∞∞

SIXTEEN

It is solitary drinking that makes drunkards.
—Nathaniel West.

The next morning Olivia and I set out to visit the hotel. Claire's three children, William, Robert and Shirley greeted us on the lawn outside the front entrance. Their regular visit to Kweetsa fell on the final weekend of each month. They loved to visit with their mother for a few days respite from the school in Pietersburg. Claire's mother, along with her new husband James, looked after them and saw to all their needs.

Hello, Uncle Tom," they called in unison. "Mommy's in the kitchen."

I smiled and left Olivia to chat with them. She loved the children and loved to tell them stories about her parent's farm.

Claire came out of the kitchen and wiped food-soiled hands on her apron. "I want to kill Old Cronje," she cried.

"What's he done now?" I asked.

"He went off to the butchery and forgot the pot of soup on the stove—it's boiled over and fifty per-cent is lying on the floor. I have the servants cleaning it up. What can I do for you, Tom?"

"We need to talk."

She raised her eyebrows.

"We can sit in the dining room. It's not time to prepare for the luncheon yet," she said.

We sat on the settee and I off-loaded my long, sad story. While I used every vulgar adjective available to my limited vocabulary, in description of Robert King's character, she sat with quiet dignity and waited for me to finish. I twiddled my fingers and waited to be scolded with a, "I told you so," but it never came.

Instead, she sighed and looked at me with empathy. "Now you know why I didn't want to sign the contract—there's just something false about this pompous Mr. King."

She placed her hand on my wrist but I couldn't look her in the eye.

"I'm sorry, Claire. I've screwed up big time. Vermeulen, the lawyer, said I could lose the farm and the mineral rights if I don't come up with the money to continue—however, if I do manage to find capital to support the operation, it means throwing good money after bad."

"If you lose the farm I'll need to find another supplier of beef and venison but don't worry I'm sure we can work something out. They're trying to force you into bankruptcy. This is most unfortunate for you, Thomas."

"I feel so trapped. If Will had been here—"

Claire reached up and stroked my cheek in sympathy. "Don't worry, we'll think of something."

I took her hand in mine, on the verge of tears. "Please forgive me—I should have listened to you."

"Think positive, Thomas. I'll make some enquiries with a friend I have in Pietersburg—we'll work it out."

Olivia arrived in the lounge with the children and I let go of Claire's hand. Liv's eyes showed a sudden distress, the well-meant gesture by Claire miss-interpreted as a carnal familiarity. She greeted Claire with a nod. "Thomas, is your business done?"

"Yes, Claire and I have discussed the situation."

"Can we go, please?" I detected a tear in one of her eyes.

I thanked Claire for the chat and stood to go. We said our farewells to the children, mounted up on the horses and rode back to the farm in silence. I could have kicked myself. I should not have sat next to Claire on the settee but chosen one of the chairs instead—too late now!

Letsatsi brought lunch out onto the veranda. I lit up a cigarette, blew a cloud of smoke into the warm afternoon air and waited for Olivia to sound off at me. We ate in silence for a while before the thick atmosphere became too much to bare.

"It didn't mean anything, Liv."

She made no attempt to answer.

I tried again. "We were only discussing the problem. Claire told me not to worry and we would find a way."

"Don't lie Thomas. I saw her stroke your cheek and you kissed her hand. I know she is in love with you—always has been."

My frustrations surfaced. "Claire loved Willy-John with all her heart while he lived. She has never indicated anything to the contrary."

"Buckpoop, Thomas. I see how she looks at you. She may have lost her husband but perhaps she sees you as a replacement."

"You have it all wrong, Liv. Claire is just one of those touchy people—she loves to touch those whom she talks to. You've seen her do it on many an occasion."

"But she has a special touch for you, Thomas. I see it in her eyes. A woman knows these things."

"I will not sit here and be falsely accused," I said. "I'm going for a walk."

"Don't forget to take your gun with you—you might as well shoot me at the same time," she said.

"Now you're talking utter tripe, Olivia."

She jumped up, stormed to the bedroom and slammed the door.

"Not again," I mumbled. Her jealous nature irritated the life out of me.

With the rifle and a bottle of Brandy in hand I headed down the verandah steps and made for the dig-site. The dogs looked up and thumped their tails on the floor as I passed by.

"You Stupid, bloody dogs don't know anything. You're both even too chicken to accompany me out onto the farm."

I never understood what Willy-J saw in them —large, lethargic animals. Consumed a ton of meat and slept for twenty hours a day. In frustration I gave the nearest dog a kick with my boot and they both jumped up to slink off into the house.

The site, quiet and deserted, reminded me of a cemetery. The rocks looked like giant tombstones and the excavation areas like open graves. I thought of the four-hundred tons of crystal, sitting on the docks in London. It crossed my mind to have the entire shipment dumped in the Thames, to alleviate the costs.

I sat down next to the steam hammer, lit up another cigarette and took a long swig from the brandy bottle. With every successive swig my troubles drifted further away until my thoughts gave precedence to Olivia's final words about Claire and I. I know men can be very naïve when it comes to the attentions paid to them by other women but maybe Liv's intuition held some water. By the time the bottle fell empty from my shaky hand the conviction of Claire's love for me became entrenched in my psyche. Such a fine fellow as I, after all said and done—a good catch, except for my married status—but even this appeared to be a trivial detail.

I picked up the empty bottle, threw it into the veld and shouted profanities at Robert King. My marriage also came under violent condemnation as did my inability to make a go of the Mine. The Afrikaners have a good saying for someone in my state: Dronkverdriet; "drunken grief." The brandy brought all my inhibition and insecurity to the surface; a worthless idiot who should have died in the place of his brother. I contemplated the use of the Mauser—to put an end to the misery but fell asleep instead.

Later, I awoke to a familiar sound. My foot appeared to be caught up by a creature which proceeded to pull my leg outwards. I thought at first it might be another dream but the notion soon dispelled when the familiar sound got louder.

With a sudden start my eyes focused to see two small, green lights, close together and part of a dark object, which pulled with tenacity at my foot. The lights turned out to be the eyes of a wild animal on its foray for food. The hyena's firm grip and occasional shake of the head woke me up. A quick glance around revealed a dangerous situation. A dozen or more eyes glinted in the semidarkness, like ghosts on a moonlit parade. The familiar laugh and jabber made by the hyenas, filtered through into my foggy state and changed my perception from wakeful inebriation to instant sobriety.

I grabbed the rifle and raised it to fire a warning shot to scare the beast away. The Mauser responded with a loud "crack" and the hyena holding my foot let go with a frightened yelp. My action, however, achieved the desired result and the pack evaporated into the night.

A sudden lurch-and-heave sensation followed and I pitched forward to retch over the Steam hammer cover. If the pack attacked with one accord there would have been no chance of my survival but hyenas tend to be cautious animals, hence my fortunate escape.

∞∞

SEVENTEEN

Drinking makes such fools of people, and people are such fools to begin with... —Robert Benchley.

The farmhouse lay bathed in the moonlight, its dark, thatched roof in stark contrast to the white-washed mud-plastered walls. All looked so peace-ful.

To my surprise an empty bedroom greeted me. The undisturbed bed-linen suggested Liv's possi-ble departure from the homestead. I wandered around, and called her name but the house gave up none of its secrets. I noticed the absence of a rifle from the gun-rack and thought she might be out in the backyard but a quick glance through the kitchen window dispelled the notion.

The lounge side-board produced the answer to my question in the form of a note written in Olivia's hand.

Dear husband,

I don't know what is happening to us. We seem to be fighting more than ever and I'm not sure who, or what, is to blame. I have taken the 303 for protection and am heading to my parent's farm for a period of time. I am sure we will eventually work this all out, but for now, I need my space.

Your loving wife,
Olivia.

I sat down on the couch in front of the fireplace. The paper felt smooth as I rubbed it between thumb and forefinger—the fragrance of her perfume wafted up from the sheet and I closed my eyes for a moment to savor it. What should I do—go out to Trichardt in the morning and ask her to return with me? My stomach still felt tender from all the brandy and my head throbbed with pain. A quick glance at the right boot revealed the hyena's teeth marks, but for the Mauser, the circumstance might have been quite different.

I stalked off to the bathroom for a quick wash-up. The empty house reverberated with silence as I stretched out on the bed to catch up on much needed sleep.

*

Days passed without word from Olivia. I occupied myself with several chores which included collection of firewood for the stove in the kitchen. I also sat down with a book of poems, one Willy-J used to read for relaxation.

On several occasions, a trip to the Potgieter's farm became a strong consideration but due to pride I baulked at the idea. She left me and she should be the one to return. A glance at the kitchen calendar revealed the duration of one week since her departure. For the first time the thought crossed my mind—she may not come back.

One late afternoon, much to Letsatsi's chagrin, I decided to ride over to the hotel for a drink. With the larder's supply of brandy depleted, the bar at the hotel's saloon provided the remaining option. She rebuked me several times over the days about the habit, but I let her know in no uncertain terms, no one gave me orders.

The hotel always bustled with patrons over a weekend, filled with travelers on route between Beit Bridge and Pretoria. The saloon, full of thirsty travelers celebrated the night stop-over with laughter and music, accompanied by the piano in the corner. Intrigued by the songs I pushed through the crowd to see Claire in action on the ivories, oblivious to all the ardent admirers around her. With a drink from the bar in hand and instructions to old Cronje to keep an eye out for my empty glass, I plonked myself at her elbow, to pick up on the song with gusto.

A few songs later she took a break and we moved to a corner table for a chat. I wanted to hear the Pietersburg family's latest news and catchup on the latest performance of the businesses.

"The children are all fine. William and Robert are doing well at school but Shirley struggles with the discipline. She has a mind of her own, that one," Claire said.

I remembered an incident when Shirley, four years old, tried to climb up to the top shelf of the home's larder to get at a jar of sugar-biscuits. The jar tumbled down to break on the floor. She screamed for help. Will punished her but she tried again, not once but two more times, before Claire hid the jar in another place. Shirley took no heed of most disciplinary instruction and also declined well-meant cautionary advice—as a result trouble found her on a regular basis. We laughed about the many times Willy-J tried to stop her from sneaking out at night, to sit on the farm verandah and look at the stars.

I ordered some more brandy and the conversation continued until Claire stood up. "I must play again—are you going to be on your way?"

"I'll finish off my drink first," I said. "Perhaps we can talk again during your next break if I'm not too drunk."

She frowned. "It's not like you to drink so much, Tom. Is something bothering you?"

"Olivia has left me."

She sat down again with a concerned look on her face. "Have you two argued again—what is happening?"

I tried to keep the tears back but failed. Claire pulled her chair around to my side of the table and put her arm around my shoulders. "I can see you're upset but surely she will come back?"

I wiped the tears from my eyes in embarrassment. The brandy effected my emotions to the point my voice sounded all choked. "I've been so miserable."

She kissed my forehead and stood. "I must get back to the piano—don't go yet. We can talk during my next break."

I relaxed and continued to sip on my glass of brandy while she played soft, moody music for about thirty minutes, at which time Old Cronje made an announcement with regards to the train's departure. True to tradition the engine driver gave three short blasts on the whistle.

I glanced at the clock above the fireplace and wondered if Claire might allow me to sleep in the hotel for the night. My legs felt shaky from all the alcohol and to ride Dreamer in such a condition constituted a danger to my safety. Many of the patrons payed up their tabs and said goodbye to friends. Claire came back to the table and sat down. She called to Cronje for a glass of water. He cast me a worried look and returned to the bar.

"When last did you speak to Olivia, Thomas?"

"Over a week ago—we had an argument over a trivial thing and she left while I was out on a walk."

"Have you stopped the mining operation completely?"

"There's no point in continuing without funds. The bank refuses to give me an overdraft."

"So—when do you think The CBF will foreclose on your lease and mineral rights?"

"Soon. I don't know what to do."

"You should go out and shoot all the venison you can. I can at least pay you for it."

"I have told Polo to continue bringing in all the vegetables and I will bring in your venison needs until I am forced off the land. Thank you for being so understanding, Claire."

My words started to slur. The room spun around a few times and I shut my eyes. "Can I sleep here tonight?"

"I will get Meisie to fix up a bed in the outhouse for you—unfortunately all the hotel rooms are full."

I stood to my feet as Claire came around the table to help me. I staggered out through the lobby to the back of the hotel with her in support and into the outhouse which served as extra storage. She held onto me as I sagged down onto an unmade bed in the corner. I took advantage of her inability to support my full weight and pulled her down on top of me.

I kissed her on the lips and held onto her as she struggled to regain an upright position. "No,

Thomas! You're drunk and you are a married man."

"I don' give-a-hootch. I wantshoo, Claire—you're sho beaushiful," I slurred.

She managed to wrench free from my grasp and stood at the door, shaken. "Sleep it off, Thomas—and make sure you're gone by the time I get up. I don't want to see you again."

Her sudden anger seeped through into my befuddled state. "Pleashe Claire—don be crosh wish me—I luv you sho mush...."

The door slammed and I heard the crunch of gravel under her footsteps as she made for the hotel's back door. Silence reigned for a few brief moments before I passed out.

∞∞

EIGHTEEN

A bend in the road is not the end of the road,
unless you fail to make the turn. — *Unknown.*

The next morning brought the rays of the sun in through the storerooms single, high window. I awoke with a jolt, confused and at a loss with the surroundings, before memory of the previous evening returned.

Claire's final words still rang in my brain—I tried to remember what preceded her anger but it all swirled together in a mist of uncertainty—a principle must have been overstepped so I decided to leave poste-haste.

My head throbbed, a condition which appeared to be on the increase in recent times. Dreamer turned his head and cast a sleepy eye when I entered the stable to saddle up. Claire must have put him to bed. The ride back to the farm caused my head to throb more violently and several times I almost fell of Dreamer's back. The horse knew his master well—if my body leaned too far over on either side he would stop in order to jar me back to semi-wakefulness.

Letsatsi glared at me with large, round eyes as I fell off Dreamer's back, and hit my head on the ground. She rushed out to help but I shooed her away with several swear words. After a struggle to stay upright, climb the verandah steps and negotiate the passageway into the bedroom, Letsatsi, managed to maneuver me onto the bed where she left me face down and clothed, to sleep.

I awoke several hours later with a concerned Polo on the bed next to me.

"Morena him dlink too mush?"

I acknowledged his concerns and took my head in my hands with a groan.

He held out a glass of strange colored liquid.

"Morena dlink dis."

I wondered what African concoction he wanted me to imbibe.

"What are you giving me, Polo?"

"Morena dlink—fix stomik."

I took the glass and swallowed the contents. It tasted vile. I jumped up from the bed and with great effort managed to keep the contents of my stomach. In the race to reach the long-drop john, outside before puking, I tripped and fell. The fermented brandy all came out in one shot on the passage floor. I must admit I felt a little better.

"God, Polo—you're trying to kill me," I said.

"Morena feel betta now?"

"Remind me not to ever have you cook dinner."

"Ee, Morena—Polo, him good cook."

I left it at that.

Later in the morning I managed to find my way out onto the verandah for a cigarette and flopped down into one of the chairs. The dogs acknowledged my presence with the usual thump, thump of the tail and went back to sleep. A minute later one of them raised his head and sat up with ears tuned to a distant sound. Several moments later a horseman galloped up to the home. I recognized him as the regional postman, who from time to time delivered important documents from Trichardt and Pietersburg, to our small business community.

"Hello, Hans. What brings you to my doorstep on this fine day?"

Hello, Mister Satherwaite. I have a document for you. It comes from England."

My heart fell—at a guess, a letter from CBF. I took it from him and opened it.

"It can only be bad news," I said.

"Aagh, I'm sorry to be the bearer then, Mr. Satherwaite." Hans's heavy Afrikaans accent always fascinated me. I could sense his empathy.

The letter, written on the company's letter head, sprouted legalese from the get-go. It stressed the need for me to vacate the farm by a certain date or risk eviction by force. The two signatures below belonged to Robert King and one of his superiors.

"Thank you, Hans. Give my best to your wife and kids."

"Thank you, Mr. Satherwaite." He turned the horse and galloped back down the path, toward the road.

I stood and stared after him until the dust from the horses hooves settled. The letter contained a directive—three months to come up with another four tons of corundum. The absence of further supply constituted a violation of the agreement and seizure of all my assets. What a ludicrous situation—four hundred tons sat on the docks in England without a market and now the company asked for another full delivery.

Hopelessness overtook me, plus the need for another drink. After a thorough search through the kitchen and larder I remembered the brandy stockpile no longer existed and nor did I have any money. Claire's words about the supply of venison to the butchery came to mind—maybe meat could be traded for brandy and food. The thought of a walk in the open veld appealed to me but I remembered an Afrikaans idiom: "More is nog n dag!" Translated it means, "Tomorrow is another day." Today, I still suffered a severe hangover—a clear head is required on a hunt. I would gather Polo and a few of his cronies in the morning and go look for venison.

*

A week later I sat with old Cronje at the hotel bar counter. Claire and I buried the hatchet after my profuse apologies with regards to the evening of my drunken advances. She remained reserved, however, and reminded me in no uncertain terms that Willy-John never tolerated such behavior on my behalf. If I ever did it again she would ban me from the hotel.

I received my rebuke with grace—I deserved it. Besides she held the purse strings. The proceeds of the hunt received more than adequate compensation, a consideration I took with much gratitude. My sister-in-law, although unhappy with my behavior, still cared for me. I made up my mind to behave in a correct manner toward her at all future times.

Olivia remained cool toward me and I later found out someone at the hotel reported on my drunken impropriety—my inebriated exit from the saloon with Claire as support, did neither of us any great honor.

A familiar voice at my elbow caught my attention. "Hello Mr. Satherwaite, how are you?"

I turned to face the speaker. Pieter Vermuelen, the lawyer from Louis Trichardt smiled at me over his glass.

"What brings you to Kweetsa, Mr. Vermeulen,"I asked.

"Actually, since you ask, I have come on behalf of a client."

"How is your practice doing?"

He downed the drink, turned his head to old Cronje and asked for another. "Business is looking up, Mr. Satherwaite."

"Call me Tom," I said. "And who might this client be?"

His eyes twinkled followed by the hint of a smile. "Now that you ask, Mr. Satherwaite, I can't say because it's confidential but I can tell you who this client wants me to represent."

"Oh—this secret client is asking you to represent a third party?"

"That's correct, Sir."

"Please call me, Tom."

"Sorry, sir—I mean—Tom."

I liked the young fellow. He seemed forthright and his words intrigued me. "So, who is this lucky person you are going to assist?"

"I am looking at him."

"You are wanting to represent me in the Corundum case?"

"Yes—you are a most fortunate soul, Tom. My client has said I am to give you as much assistance in fighting this company as will be required to bring about a just solution."

"But didn't you tell me the other day this company has an iron-clad case against me?"

"Not in so many words—I knew you possessed no funds to put up a defense and I, much to my chagrin, cannot spend time doing it Pro-bono."

"Who is this mystery client?"

"I'm afraid I can't say—"

"I know. You've already said it's confidential, however, I will never allow myself to receive charity."

"Oh, this will not be charity, Tom. I can assure you my client will allow you to pay back every penny I have charged when we are successful."

"You sound as if you know something about this case."

"I know if you turn this offer down you'll lose your farm and a chance at making your fortune."

My mind spun in opposite directions in an attempt to digest Vermeulen's words. I wondered if Olivia might have taken pity on me and asked her father for a loan. I couldn't think of anyone else who might have the available funds, but Mr. Potgieter given my history, would never risk it on me. Someone must have seen an opportunity to make a fortune from the corundum—perhaps a rich miner from the Reef?

I thought for a few moments. "Tell your client I accept on the condition I will pay back every penny if we are successful. If, however, we fail, he cannot expect anything in return."

"My client will ask for nothing in the case of my failure. You have nothing to fear. You will be a part of the solution, though."

"A part of the solution?"

"You will be taking a trip to England."

NINETEEN

Once you choose hope, anything is possible.
—Christopher Reeve

Vermeulen's words did not sink in at first. The whole discussion seemed too much like a fairytale and I wanted to pinch myself to make sure it wasn't a dream. A sniff at my drink confirmed Old Cronje did not pour me a foreign concoction.

"A trip to England is a costly affair. I don't have any funds."

"We know your financial predicament, Tom. My client will carry all the costs—you will stay in London and work with an acquaintance."

"Who is this...acquaintance?"

Let's just say he is a friend of a friend, who will be willing to help you find your way around London's darker side. I would not call him a private eye— perhaps more of a 'gatherer of information', is closer to the truth. My client will pay his fare."

The offer of support from this mysterious client, bordered on the surreal.

"To afford such expenses your client must have deep pockets," I said.

Vermuelen gave me a thin smile. "Don't concern yourself about money. This acquaintance will assist you in finding what you are looking for—documents, contracts, incriminating evidence of the company's illegal intensions."

"You are suggesting we sleuth around their offices in an illegal type of way?"

"You must fight fire with fire, Tom—but don't tell anyone I told you to do anything illegal. You will have to be extremely careful. Patch Foster will give you whatever assistance you require but it will be up to you to recognize any illegal stuff you discover."

I frowned. "Patch Foster?"

"He is the acquaintance I told you about. Not exactly the most sophisticated person but one who knows the area and the people involved."

"What happens to the farm in my absence?"

"Your overseer, Mr. Polo, will run things under my supervision. I understand he is loyal to you?"

"Polo is the only real friend I have—come to think of it he is a good hunter and should be able to keep the contract with the butchery in good shape. I can trust him with my life."

Vermeulen took another sip from his glass. "You are not to tell anyone about my client's offer or the mission to England. It must remain a secret between us."

"Agreed. Let's drink to your client—and to success," I said.

He raised his glass and gulped down the remainder of its contents. "I will arrange your passage to England and money will be wired to a bank of my client's choice. You must use the funds sensibly and conclude your business within three weeks of your arrival there."

It all came down to me with a sudden fearful thought: I didn't have a clue what to do on my arrival in the Old Country. Talk about a fish out of water.

"This is all very grand but is your client not placing too much faith in my ability?"

"You will have some assistance, Tom but Patch will go over a plan of action with you."

Vermeulen's explanation didn't evoke much comfort but he seemed confident regarding the outcome.

"When do I leave?"

"I will visit you at the farm tomorrow to tie up the loose ends. Tell your overseer you are taking a vacation, going to see your family, whom I presume still live there. You will need to leave the day after tomorrow."

"What about my ticket for the passage to England?"

"By the time your train arrives in Cape Town your ticket will be ready and waiting at the Union Castle Line offices."

I stood to leave and extended my hand. "Until tomorrow, then?"

"I will see you at midday." He shook my hand and I left the bar. Claire, busy with some patrons at the reception, waved as I passed by the front entrance. I waved back and smiled, desperate to tell her about the turn in my fortunes, but Vermeulen's request for secrecy came to mind.

Dreamer whinnied and stamped a hoof, eager to get back to the farm—I felt almost buoyant—a positive turn in events.

*

Polo and Letsatsi greeted the news of my vacation with the acceptance and respect they always showed when I shared news with them. They considered me to be a part of their village family and treated me like a father.

"Morena, him go see mme?" said Letsatsi. I could tell she considered a visit to my mother a righteous deed.

Polo, I could see, relished the idea of the farm's management while I visited with family in England. He promised to keep the butchery in good supply of beef, milk and venison. Above all he treasured oversight of the Mauser. The farm would be in good hands.

Pieter Vermeulen arrived the next day as promised and we sat on the verandah, each with a cup of coffee. He outlined the company's scope of operation and told me what to look out for. Mention of my contact's name, "Patch" Foster, intrigued me—a strange first name. The benefactor required my expense money to be wired to a bank in London and made available to me at my convenience. Pieter's mother, his chief cook and bottle washer took care of all the administration and he assured me all would be in order on my arrival in the great city, as per his client's instructions.

"I don't know how to thank you, Pieter."

"It's my client you will be thanking, after all this is taken care of," he said.

He left at three pm, in a carriage drawn by a single horse. He waved goodbye without a turn of the head. I wondered about his age—his client must have great confidence in his abilities to trust him with such an endeavor. I shrugged my shoulders and strode off around the back of the house to the storeroom to search for the suitcases Willy-J and I first used on our epic trip to the region.

Later, I sat out on the verandah and considered a note to Olivia. No contact in almost three weeks implied the presence of a failed marriage and in case she decided to pay me a sudden visit it might be expedient for her to know no a reason for my absence. A short note of explanation written by the light of the oil lantern in the lounge and placed on the mantle above the fireplace, settled the question.

A good supply of ammunition for Polo's excursions lay stacked on the shelf in the larder, accompanied by matches and lantern oil for Letsatsi, who would stay in the house. Out of respect she refused to use any of the three bedrooms and brought in a mattress to place on the kitchen floor. An excitement gripped me and several sleepless hours passed before slumber came.

*

The train left Kweetsa station at ten-thirty the next morning. Polo drove the small carriage, drawn by an indignant Dreamer, to the station and deposited me with two suitcases at the steps of the platform. We stood about for a while and when the time arrived for the train to depart, I could see the tears in his eyes. "Morena look uftah selluf."

I hugged him, an action he never got used to, picked up my suitcases and walked onto the platform. The steam-engine stood parked in front of three coupled carriages. It belched out puffs of smoke from the stack and dispelled condensate from the over-pressurized cylinders which drove the wheels. The trip by train, from Cape Town to Pretoria with Willy-J and the family, filled my memory.

At least eight years of history now separated the present day from those idyllic times and my brown hair showed some distinct grey strands. I felt much older than my thirty-one years, a testimony to the harshness of bush-life and the onset of recent problems.

The trip to Cape Town took ten days and on arrival at the Union Castle line offices near the docks, my penchant for train-travel died a miserable death. The sub-standard food, consolidated with boredom took its toll of my patience but increased my eagerness to get on the ship for England. Old memories flooded back at the sight of Table Mountain and Lion's Head, the most distinguished landmarks of the City's backdrop.

Without incident the ship left Cape Town harbor and I said goodbye to the beloved land, comforted in the knowledge that when I next set eyes on the city, my life should have taken a turn for the better. Twelve days later the ship steamed into London harbor—ready to begin the next chapter of my saga.

∞∞

TWENTY

The real voyage of discovery consists not in seeking new landscapes but in having new eyes. —Marcel Proust.

Many people stood in the Castle Line's reception area as the passengers disembarked. I scrutinized those who waited for family or fares, in the hope of an advanced handle on Patch Foster. Vermeulen had mentioned few details, except an assurance of his presence at the docks on the day of my arrival.

Perhaps the omission came by absentmindedness or design, it didn't matter much—it's good to make up one's own mind about others. Two people remained in the aftermath of all the happy embraces, hugs and arm-slaps which followed the disembarkation of the remaining passengers and I assumed one of them must be Foster.

I chose the mustachioed man dressed in a pinstriped suit, with round-shaped spectacles and umbrella. He appeared to assume the character of a private eye, perhaps in some form of disguise. Smiling at the man I picked up both my cases, stepped over and posed the question: "Mr. Foster?"

The man looked down his nose at me and shook his head. "I'm not your man, Sir."

Puzzled, my eyes swiveled toward the second person, slouched against a roof-support pillar. This fellow appeared to be the most improbable choice to represent the interests of my benefactor. Vermeulen's vague description of 'not the most sophisticated person' came to mind. An over-sized cap sat draped, in precarious fashion over his head, as though someone might have tossed it onto a hat-stand without thought. The baggy clothes made me think of a circus clown. A cigarette dangled from his lips and in an instant I understood the tag of "Patch." A black eye-patch, hidden by the cap, covered the left eye. I thought of Long John Silver, the fictional pirate in Robert Louis Stevenson's Treasure Island, a copy of which Willy-J once boasted ownership as a teenager.

"Mr. Foster?"

"At yer service, Govner."

The commoner accent gave his background away and I shuddered. How on earth could anyone work with such a creature?

Patch slouched forward and stuck out a grimy paw. Afraid I might need a dose of penicillin to ward off infections, I hesitated to take the hand. What on earth made Vermeulen think this slum-dweller could be of any help to me? My hasty judgements of Foster would soon be dispelled when business got underway.

"Av a good trip, Govner?"

I sighed with a discontentment. "Certainly long and boring."

"No matter, Guv. I'll gets yer to the board-in'ouse wheres yer'll be stayen and you can enjoy a bit o shutoi."

"Thank you, er, Mr. Foster."

He grabbed one of my suitcases, flicked the cigarette into the gutter and made off down the corridor toward the exit.

"Jus call me Patch, Guv—every'un else duz."

"I'll remember that."

We exited into a busy street where I learned with alacrity pedestrians subsisted as an afterthought. The age of the auto, even more so than Cape Town, ruled supreme and the streets saw few horse-drawn carriages. But for Cape Town and Durban, not many 'internal combustions' existed in the Northern areas of South Africa, certainly not between Pretoria and Southern Rhodesia. Most people in the rural areas did not even know about them.

We needed to cross the road to hail a taxi.

"Mind ow yer go, Guv. Wouldn' do to be scrapin ya off th'groun."

Patch's caution came in good time as a tram bore down on us at full speed. I dodged out of the way and marveled at how things tended to change since the turn of the century.

Foster hailed a taxi and it pulled in to where we stood. The wheels missed my feet by one or two inches. We lifted the suitcases onto the rack above the boot at the rear of the vehicle and climbed in. Patch gave directions.

"Th' Orse's Ed, and make it snappy, mate."

My temporary home, an establishment called the Horses Head, sounded creepy—the taxi driver jumped the clutch and caused the vehicle to lurch forward like an angry bull as we took off, followed by a cloud of black smoke. Fifteen minutes later we chugged into the drive of a red-brick, Victorian building which must have been over sixty years old.

"I know it don look much, Guv but tis cheap enough for a longish stay."

"I'll take your word for it." I hoped the 'longish' stay remained purely metaphorical.

"Food's good too, Guv—yer'll be appy'ere."

I nodded; my first impressions threatened an attack of depression. Dear God, preserve me.

The driver parked and we climbed down off the running-board to retrieve my suitcases. Patch stopped and looked at me. The driver waited with his arm out of the window and hand extended—I realized they wanted me to pay the fee. I carried several pound notes in my pocket so I handed over a note to the driver. He looked at me and grinned. "Thanks, Matey."

I waited for my change but he dropped the clutch and took off at speed.

"Bugger," said Patch. "Ya gotta lern the fees, Guv. Neva giv' em a note."

"I'll remember for the next time," I said.

We picked up the suitcases and walked into the reception. A gaunt, elderly man glared at us from behind the counter and cleared his throat.

"Lookin for a room, then?"

Patch smiled and doffed his cap. He turned to me and said, "Mr. Satherwaite 'ere as a room booked, mate."

The old clerk eyed me over as though my presence suggested a need to hide the crown jewels.

"Does he, then? Let's 'ave a gander at the register. Ah yes, I see a Mr. Satherwaite on the list." He reached over to a board on which several keys hung, snapped one off a hook and threw it on the counter.

"Room seven—you'll find it down the corridor, to the left. Check the notice on the back o' your door—eatin' times are exactly what you read there. No noise after ten and before six in the 'mornin."

He turned and walked off into an adjacent office as though we never existed. I looked at Patch who inclined his head and smiled. "Take'em as 'ey cum, Guv."

I realized how different South Africans behaved. The British came across as arrogant and rude, a fact long forgotten due to my absence.

Patch put the suitcase down and turned to leave. "I'll be'ere at eight temorrah, Guv. We'll concoct a game plan and make sum desishuns."

I thanked him for his help and said goodbye. One look around the room revealed a single bed and small table, a desk with chair and a loose-standing cupboard—not much to write home about. Not even a rug on the floor. I sat on the bed to test the mattress—a host of lumps and bumps. The center formed into a crevice and I imagined the struggle to extricate self, come the morning. No doubt, my mysterious benefactor slept in a fine bed, drank fine wine every night and gave no thought to any comforts for his chosen vassal.

Guilt flushed out my antagonistic thoughts in a sudden surge of self-reproach—this same benefactor footed the bills. A glance at my latest purchase, a cheap pocket-watch, showed the time to be 6:20pm. The notice on the back of the door indicated dinner to start at 6:00pm and end at 8.

Desperate to use the john my first foray into the rest of the building took me down a passageway, past six rooms and out through a door into the backyard. A smaller abode with a sign, "Bathrooms and Toilets," greeted me. Inside, the lights came on at a flick of a switch, gadgetry to get used to—no electricity existed Kweetsa—the lanterns and candles posed the typical ambiance of our life in the bush. To set up a lantern, fill it with oil and strike the match to light the wick, represented a bygone age; all now became available at the flick of a switch and I'm not sure I liked it.

The dining hall needed a fresh coat of paint to brighten the place up a bit but the general feel of the room commanded a measure of respectability. We ate regular beef, a far cry from the gamey taste of venison my pallet enjoyed, supplemented with veggies and potatoes. I found Patch's comment about the food to be accurate. I enjoyed the meal but my satisfaction might have been more hunger driven. The dinner ended with a dessert, fit for a king and I left for my room contented. After a shower in the outhouse the lumpy bed didn't seem so bad after all and I fell asleep within minutes.

∞∞

TWENTY-ONE

It takes two flints to make a fire.   —L.M. Alcott.

Morning came in concert with the strange noises of my new locality. A quick glance at the pocket-watch on the small, bedside table showed 6:10 am.

I decided to resist the temptation of a lie-in, slipped out of the bed and stumbled across the room to the window, for a quick look at the outside surroundings. A grass lawn rested under the canopy of several tall trees and a brick wall marked the boundary of the property's back yard—picturesque and peaceful. An urgent need to use the john pulled my attention away from the scenic vista and focused on the stand-alone cupboard to retrieve my dressing gown. The door required a hard yank on the handle before it opened, a legacy of the moisture from London's incessant rainfall.

Breakfast would be convened at seven so I hustled on my gown and made for the outhouse shower. Nobody else appeared to be up. Later, dressed and hungry, I could smell the aroma of scrambled eggs as I took my seat.

"Mornin, Guv."

Patch Foster stood at the door of my room with a toothy grin. He wore the same clothes; baggy soiled pants, a crinkled white shirt with frayed collar and an old no-name-brand jacket, with lapel turned up. The over-sized cap slanted downward at an angle, covered the black eye-patch.

"Good morning, Patch—where can we sit to discuss business?"

"Small pub roun-th'corner Govner—good place for a pint."

I couldn't imagine beer consumption in the morning but perhaps my new friend's habits reflected the norm for his status in life. I nodded and we walked out of the building toward the street. A few minutes later we seated ourselves in a dingy dive of a place. Patch shouted to the bartender, whom he appeared to know, for two pints of beer and our business got underway.

"What is it you do for a living, Patch?"

"I doo a bit o'this and a bit o' that, Guv, but mainly I collect informaishun for people."

I thought about Patch's answer and recalled Vermeulen's description. The title of 'collector of information' seemed a little vague but perhaps apt so I let it go—figured the lawyer knew more than I did.

"Mr. Vermeulen suggested you know your way around London and are familiar with the CBF company —the one with which we have an issue."

"I knows em well, Guv—been doin ma'own 'slewfin."

"Sleuthing," I suggested. I could see I might need an interpreter for future dialogues.

"Yeah, as I sed, Guv—'slewfin."

"What have you discovered so far?"

"Yor pal, Mistah King, is ah—well connected. I's bin follow'n im round fer sum time. E 'as cunnecshuns to a real bad un, e' as—a hoity-toity, polytishun, if I might say it outright."

The news didn't surprise me; Robert King, my nemesis, kept company with a politician. "We have to find something on King—something I can use against him. What about the company?"

"Ah, the company," said Patch. Tis run by a bad 'un—calls 'im-self Mister Ex. Real name is J.S Wilcox—John Sebastian Wilcox."

"What have you discovered about the operation?"

"Theys inta the Protectshun Racket, Guv. Extorshun an Racketeerin as such, and Mister Ex is also well-connectud—e's in the parlyment."

It dawned on me. "Oh, that John Sebastian Wilcox."

I remembered from my previous existence, a parliamentarian by this name. The news did not bode well. If one so high up in the government held the gun to my head it I doubted my ability to take such a person down.

"How well do you know the company's main office? Is there any chance of staging a break-in to search for incriminating records?"

"Tis on my list, Guv. I'll need yer 'elp tho."

"When, and what time?"

"Tonight, 'bout ten."

I shuddered. Break-in and enter did not gel well with me but to find evidence for incrimination of the company, it needed to be done. Patch finished his beer and wiped the foam off his lips with the back of a grimy hand. I left my tankard half full and as we got up to leave he stopped and looked at my beer. I nodded and he gulped the remainder down with a smack of the lips.

The bar tender eyed me for payment. This time I remembered Patch's advice—no notes. A quick scrounge in my wallet produced two shillings which I placed in the tender's hand. He grinned and I believed I held the short end of the stick again.

We walked back to the boarding house and a quick glance at the pocket watch suggested lunch to be served within the hour.

"You'll be around at ten tonight?"

"I'll pick yer up, Guv. Wearsum dark cloves."

∞∞

TWENTY-TWO

Out of the frying pan, into the fire.   —John Heywood.

Patch and I walked down Leadenhall Street toward the CBF offices. Positioned a block from the famous White Star Lines offices the Company's building, built with old red-bricks, posed a contrast to the more modern structures of the central London, commercial zone.

My colleague, who knew his way around the area, turned down a dark alley next to the premises and we headed toward the rear of the building. I recalled my time with the Cape Town Police. Willy-John and I often monitored the downtown shops to check for signs of break and entry. Now I found myself in violation of the same law we once upheld.

"Ere we 'ar Guv."

He stopped at the bottom of a fire escape which led upward in zig-zag fashion to the roof and motioned for me to go ahead. The steep stairs required use of the handrail to make the ascent to each landing. On arrival at the second story Patch removed a clasp knife from his trouser pocket and placed the blade under the closest window-frame. After the application of some pressure the frame shot upward and we gained access into the building. I could see he possessed a talent for this type of escapade.

Patch produced a small torch to illuminate our way and we moved down a corridor in silence and passed by several office doors, each with a name plaque. We looked for two names in particular—Robert King and R.J Wilcox.

Inscribed on the second door down, in gold letters, appeared the name of the infamous Mr. King.

"This is the one we want," I said. I couldn't believe our luck—it all seemed so easy—maybe too easy.

The door opened at the turn of the handle but I suspected Patch to be equipped to handle a lock. We moved into the office and made straight for the desk to check the contents of its drawers, which we hoped to find unlocked. Our expectations, however, fell short. No problem to Patch; as I suspected, he came prepared.

This time he produced a thin, flat blade from the seam of his coat and proceeded to work on the first drawer. A moment later I heard a click and it popped open. I asked him to focus the torch-light on the contents and lifted out a bunch of files to place on the desk for scrutiny. The first file contained the names of people, perhaps owners or managers of various companies, with whom the company did business. Columns of ticks registered against amounts of money in pounds sterling and appeared to be noted against each name. I believed the amounts to be payments for protection of property. The business of money in exchange for protection is perhaps not illegal—but cash payments reflected the intention of possible tax evasion with the money not declared as legitimate income.

I continued to look through the pile but found little more of significance. After returning the pile to the drawer I indicated for the next drawer to be unlocked. Patch obliged and more files came to light. These carried different country names, India, Portugal, Spain, the Netherlands and perhaps, not to my surprise, South Africa. The file contents revealed all sorts of contracts and paperwork for what appeared to be foreign enterprises like my own at Kweetsa.

A quick recce through the business paperwork in each of the files proved to confirm my suspicions. I left the South African file for last.

With shaky fingers I removed the contract with my signature and showed it to Patch. "This, my friend, is one of the things we are looking for."

He beamed from ear to ear and flashed a toothy grin. The shadows, cast by the torchlight created a ghoulish appearance one might expect to find in a haunted castle. What I thought of Foster before now dissolved into a quiet respect. I understood why the lawyer commissioned him for this job—there could not be many people trustworthy enough and prepared to bend the law for such a risk, although I imagined Patch might be well re-munerated for his talents. I folded the contract and placed it in my pocket.

"We need to find the big man's office," I said. J.S. Wilcox, or Mr. Ex as he referred to himself, deserved our immediate attention and I didn't want to pass up the opportunity to expose his vile enterprise.

We left King's office and crept down the hall-way to the end. Mr. Ex's workplace could have been a ballroom. Unlocked, the door led into a re-ception, prior to another room of huge propor-tions. Ornate furniture and original paintings dec-orated the floor and walls. Tall windows, hidden by long drapes, faced out to the main street-front. The desk in the center of the room must have taken several large trees to make and the executive chair put a king's throne to shame.

An upright shelf unit with glass doors caught my attention. Patch slouched over with the torch and focused on some of the contents—bound books of law. John Sebastian Wilcox, member of parliament also practiced at the law-courts as a barrister; a learned man, who subverted the very law he swore to uphold. The irony, by its sheer hypocrisy, caused me to slap my hands against my cheeks.

Patch moved to the large desk and went to work. The locked, top drawer presented no challenge for my colleague. The flat blade appeared again, wiggled about in concert with the clasp-knife and the lock submitted in defeat. I looked through the drawer's content and found a metal box with cash and a photograph of a young woman. Her face seemed familiar but I could not place it—maybe a well-known personality in London's upper social circles. The rest of the contents consisted of documents, a loaded service revolver and a small hard-covered, black book.

Patch handed the book to me and we squinted at the neat penmanship in the dull beam of the torch in an attempt to decipher the purpose. Because it needed to be locked away I deduced its value rated high in terms of required privacy. The contents of the book indicated possible sensitive information which he preferred to keep secret—this could be important for my investigation of the company.

The creak of a floorboard, outside the office door, caught our attention. We both looked toward the office entrance startled by the intrusive sound and Patch dowsed the torch. The room plunged into darkness and we both crouched next to the desk as I tried to remember the layout of the office. Suitable cover appeared limited. Patch snatched the book from my hand and melted away into the blackness, his final words—"'ide, Govner."

The door opened accompanied by the over-head light, which blinded me for a moment. A cornered rat might have scurried under the desk but no such luck for me.

"Looks like we've just won first prize' eh Bob?"

The voice sounded like a rusty old combustion engine on a cold winter's morning. I stood to my feet and rubbed my eyes until vision returned. Two men stood at the door, one with a pistol in his hand. The other, a big fellow with broad shoulders and a huge pot-belly, carried a short, wooden club. Both men appeared to be surprised to see me. I looked around for Patch but he must have found somewhere to conceal himself. I stood, frozen to the spot. My captors blocked the available exit.

The man with the pistol spoke again. "Just as well we do the rounds—isn't it, Bob?"

He raised the pistol and pointed it at my head. His short, stocky frame gave me the impression he might have fought in the ring at one time or another.

"So—what's yer case, Mister? Lookin for something to steal?"

I kept my mouth shut. No valid reason existed for my presence.

"Cat's got yer tongue, Mate?" His bloated, battle-scarred cheeks half smothered the two pig-like eyes. A jagged scar ran from the top of his fore-head down across the bridge of the flat nose and across the opposite cheek. Big Bob appeared incapable of speech and communicated his opinion via a series of grunts.

They stepped into the room, with Bob at my back and the short one in front. The blow on the back of my head came with enough force to knock out a buffalo.

*

I awoke to a sea of pain. The back of my head hurt like the devil and my ribs ached. Every small movement delivered more discomfort and for a moment I couldn't remember what had befallen me. The cold, hard floor felt like the slab of a morgue as memory filtered back, to remind me of my predicament.

I whispered Patch's name but received no reply. Did he escape? My last memory, before the two hostiles appeared at the door, included Patch, who snatched the book from my hand and told me to hide.

The darkness of the prison triggered a fear of how this escapade might end—my sudden disappearance from off the face of the Earth. Thanks to the mysterious benefactor and my lawyer, my life might be snuffed out long before we could achieve any success against the company.

I tried to roll over onto one side but the motion increased the pain in my ribs. Bob and his pal must have done a number on me. One available option remained—to wait for the morning. My captors would return to extract information. The fact of my continued existence meant my enemies intended to determine the reason for the break-in. I could bank on King or Wilcox for the next interrogation.

∞∞

TWENTY-THREE

*The supreme irony of life is that hardly any-
one gets out of it alive. —R.A Heinlein.*

I must have dozed off again. The squeak of the
door seeped through into my subconscious and
woke me up from a vivid dream. The scene of
Olivia, dressed in a skimpy gown, evaporated to be
replaced by the harsh walls of a small four by eight
room. A single, barred window, high up on the one
wall, emitted a shaft of light from the outside
world.

I blinked my eyes to dispel the residue of sleep
before my gaze fell on the figure in the doorway.

"Glad you could join us, Mate."

Scarface stared down at me with his tiny pig-
eyes. "Ope yer slept well—the boss wants to talk to
ya."

His amicable demeanor did little for the pain
in my body. I remained silent. Big Bob sauntered
in from behind Pig-eyes and lifted me off the
ground as though my body weighed zero. The
blood drained from my head and brought more
pain. Bob proceeded to push me along in front of
him, out of the cell, down a dingy corridor and up
some steps—on occasion he gave the back of my

head an extra hard shove with the palm of his hand, to emphasize his position of control.

We ended up outside a familiar door—Wilcox's office. Pig-eyes knocked and a woman's voice bade us enter. Bob pushed me ahead again as we passed through the reception to Mr. Ex's office. A vivacious girl stared at me in shock—I figured the boss kept a bevy of female assistants to aid in his crimes and boost his enormous ego.

A.J Wilcox, alias Mr. Ex, sat at his desk, one hand held by an attractive young female who manicured his fingernails. The Grey temples offset the combed, black-dyed hair, parted down the center. A pin-stripe mustache sat on his thin upper lip, like a tattoo. Well-defined cheekbones, a strong chin and a long-pointed nose completed the physical façade of his face, behind which, no doubt, an agile but devious mind existed. Several moments passed before Mr. Ex acknowledged my presence.

He looked up at me and smiled. His eyes penetrated my brain like an electric current.

"Who are you and what were you doing in my office last night?"

Wilcox's use of the upper-class English accent bore evidence of his privileged status.

"I was looking for something to steal so I could sell it," I lied.

"Colley-wobble, my dear fellow. Don't play the fool with me, sir. Do you know who I am?"

I shook my head.

"Let me tell you, then. I am John Sebastian Wilcox, a Member of Parliament and Barrister for the Crown. Ring a bell, Sir?"

Again I acted ignorant.

"Well, I'm sure Clem and Bob will get the truth out of you. You see, my good fellow, there is a very important book containing very important information, missing from my drawer."

"I didn't take your book."

"Ah—but somebody did. You were not alone, where you, sir?'"

I lowered my gaze to my feet and remained silent. I could not hide the fact of an accomplice.

Pig-eye jumped in. "Do ya need me to persuade him to talk, Mr. Wilcox?"

The possibility frightened me. Piggy tapped his fingers on the corner of Mr. Ex's desk and waited for his boss's reply.

"Hold off for a moment or two, Clem," said Wilcox. "I see the good fellow has already undergone a little hardship—maybe I can persuade him to come clean."

The door to the office burst open behind me and I wondered who else might get involved in the interrogation.

"I see you have Mr. Satherwaite in custody—how fortuitous of him to pay us a visit at this time." The voice belonged to Robert King.

I flinched and felt my knees turn to jelly. Even with tremendous verbal skills which I didn't possess, no way out of my predicament, existed. The intervention of King meant the worst kind of trouble for me—he knew the reason for my presence.

"Have you searched him?" asked King.

Pig-eyes, produced my wallet and the contract, buried in the back-pocket of my trousers. Disposal of the legal paper which held me to the company's crooked agreement, evaporated. I should have given it to Patch who somehow escaped the notice of Pig-eye and big, bad Bob—he must have hidden behind the drapes and waited for us to leave the room.

What could Patch do? Any sympathy the police might have entertained prior to our break-in ceased, compliments of our actions. There would be no reason for their empathy. A man like Wilcox, well connected with the establishment, might also have the police in his pocket. It looked bad for me.

King unfolded the contract and scrutinized it. "I see you've been into my drawers as well, Thomas."

I felt angry and embarrassed. The plan for an easy and sure way to gain control of my tenuous situation had backfired. Short of a miracle there could be no favorable outcome. I cursed Patch for the lack of information about Wilcox's guards. My appreciation of his previous achievements vanished and once again he became a low-down, tardy collector of information. To round off my thought tirade—the man absconded to save his own skin and left me with the cookie-jar.

Wilcox smiled with enthusiasm. "Well done, Robert—at least now I know why this impudent individual has committed this ill-conceived crime."

I agreed with Mr. Ex's statement. Our brilliant plan suffered serious deficiencies.

"Work him over until he comes up with his accomplice's name," said Wilcox. "Take him back to the storeroom and make sure you get the information."

Pig-eyes smiled with evil intention and rubbed his hands together while Bob grabbed the scruff of my collar and yanked me off my feet. Again he dragged me along the floor, back out into the corridor, while the astonished young receptionist looked on.

To withstand physical pain is not one of my greatest assets so I made a quick decision to spill the beans about Patch. The little, black book told its own story and someone took it, hence the irrefutable evidence of an accomplice. Bob threw me down on the cell's floor and pig-eyes waded in with the short handled, wooden club. I stuck up my arms in defense and begged him to stop—I intended to tell them what they wanted to know. The blows continued despite my obvious capitulation and I realized piggy needed his fix—to beat me within an inch of my life first, before asking for the information. No quick admission on my behalf could prevent it.

My arms soon caved in under the severity of his blows and little flashes of light sparked in my eyes as destruction rained down on my head. In a daze I collapsed onto the floor and lay on my stomach to protect my vital organs. He kept up the blows until shortness of breath caught up with him.

Silence enfolded me like a garment, even before he stopped. Yet, no plan to let me off the hook existed in the mind of my tormentor—cold water splashed down on the back of my head. Pig-eye, now with sufficient spiritual gratification, decided to allow a small window of respite. I thought of Claire, Olivia and Polo; the people I held most dear in my life and it dawned on me—I might never, in this life, see their faces again.

"So...Mr. Satherwaite. Who is your accomplice and where do we find him?"

My head throbbed and buzzed but the question came through loud and clear.

"His name is Patch Foster and I haven't a clue where you'll find him. He is a low down slouch-head who works for himself."

"And 'ow did you come by his acquaintance, Mr. Satherwaite?"

"Arranged by a lawyer who thought I could benefit from the connection."

"Where is yer lawyer situated?"

"In South Africa," I said.

Piggy paused to absorb the information. "Where does this Mr. Foster live, then?"

"I don't know—he met me at the docks when I arrived and came to my rooms at the Horse's Head, to see me yesterday. He suggested we could try to find the contract."

"Got yerself into a spot o'bother 'aven't you, Mr. Satherwaite?"

I nodded. Piggy and Bob looked at each other.

"Guess we give this information to Mr. Wilcox and let 'im decide what should be done," said pig-eyes. They moved out of the cell and left me to languish in my own blood. The door closed with a bang.

∞∞

TWENTY-FOUR

Time is limited and some opportunities never repeat themselves. —Belle de Jour.

Hours later the key engaged in the lock again, followed by a squeak of hinges, as the door swung open. Robert King looked down on me.

"You've made a grave mistake by coming here, Tom."

I stared up at his loathsome face and spat out a rebuff, my lips curled with uncontrolled hate. "It's slime like you King who should be strung up from a yard-arm and given no quarter. You pray on the ignorant and ruin lives."

King raised his chin. "We all do what we have to do, Tom. War has a way of changing people and I have learned to look after number one."

"What do you intend to do with me?"

"That's for Mr. Ex to decide but if we don't find your friend it'll turn out much worse for you."

"What information is so critical Wilcox requires so urgently?"

"It's none of your business, Satherwaite. Let's just say the information contained therein is of a very sensitive nature."

"Sensitive enough to be illegal, no doubt," I said.

*

Later in the day pig-eyes came to get me, again. This time big, bad Bob did not accompany him and I walked to Wilcox's office unaided, with the occasional shove from pig-eyes. The Boss sat behind his desk focused on a document. He ignored me for a full minute and when he spoke, his lips smiled but the eyes stared with evil intent.

"Mr. Satherwaite—shall I call you Tom?"

"You can call me whatever you want," I said.

"Okay, Tom it is, then."

I straightened up and looked him in the eye. He folded the document and placed it in a tray on the desktop.

"I understand you have a sister-in-law of whom you are very fond?" His words caused my stomach to churn.

"What of it?"

"She could get hurt in this whole thing."

"Get hurt, I don't understand," I lied.

"If Foster doesn't hand back my little black-book I will have to arrange, ah—an accident for said family member."

I felt a sudden tightness in my chest. I knew what he meant.

"I see. The problem with your intended action is I have no contact with Foster. I have no way to tell him what will happen to her."

"Foster will contact you and I will make it happen. I will set you free under surveillance, Tom. I have connections high up in Scotland Yard who will keep an eye on you."

"What am I supposed to tell Foster?"

"Tell him not to fall into temptation—not to be tempted to divulge the contents of the book. He is to have it delivered here to my office—directly to me. If it isn't in my hands by the end of the week—I will carry through on my threat. Do I make myself clear, Tom?"

"I understand," I said. I felt a weight lift off my shoulders at the thought of freedom.

"And don't think you can double-cross me. We will watch your every move. Do you understand?"

I nodded and my mind raced to figure out this sudden turn of events. Patch's disappearance may yet work in my favor. I needed to think the consequences through—Claire could not be placed at risk on my behalf.

"Am I free to go?" I asked.

"You can walk out of this office, Tom—but remember, what I have said. There will be consequences if you don't deliver."

"I will remember your words, Wilcox. Please remember mine—my sister-in-law is off limits. If one hair of her head is harmed I will come after you with everything I have."

"I appreciate your candor, Tom but the outcome is entirely in your hands."

I turned and walked out of the office, down the long corridor to the stairs. I half expected Wilcox to renege on his word and send pig-eyes after me but it didn't happen.

The bright sunlight played havoc with my sight as I exited the CBF offices and descended the steps. With one hand lifted to shade my eyes I made my way down Leadenhall Street and dodged through the pedestrian traffic, with an occasional turn of the head to see if anyone followed. On reflection of the meeting with Wilcox a tremendous sense of relief flooded my soul. The outcome might have been much worse. My body, although in severe pain and the lumps on my head, would mend—I might have been murdered. Tears of joy welled up behind my eyelids and for a moment, blinded my vision. The fresh air made me feel light-headed which caused the smile on my lips to morph into silent laughter. People raised their eyebrows in surprise at the strange behavior—my head thrown back in mirth and the unsteady gait as I weaved my way along the sidewalk.

The road down to the Horse's Head provided the first opportunity to spot the tail. I stopped and turned to look him in the eye—he smiled, touched the brim of his hat and made no effort to hide his intensions. With the unspoken acquaintance made we continued on our journey.

How will Patch contact me under the present conditions? Will he even know of my freedom?

These questions swirled around the hallways of my mind, exacerbated by the knowledge the man who followed in my wake. For the first time in twenty hours I felt hungry and the thought of a hot shower, followed by a good meal, warmed my heart.

My thoughts about Patch's character still produced a conflict but time would tell. The tail made it impossible for me to search for Foster. He would have to find me. A cable-gram as a warning for Claire and Vermeulen appeared to be a good solution but I knew Wilcox would be able to circumvent whatever arrangements I made.

The hot shower proved therapeutic but the lumps and bumps on my face felt grotesque. Bruised ribs still hurt in concert with my black and blue forearms but the thought of freedom overcame the agony of the pain.

After dinner, a walk seemed in order and I asked about the nearest grounds—a place with benches for observation of human traffic and beautiful flowers. A short way from the Horse's Head such a venue existed, as described by the old clerk at the reception. His directions led me to a large, open park with high stone walls and beautiful gardens offset by stretches of green lawn.

The cut grass and flowers smelt delightful after the smoky streets of London's downtown area. I found a bench and sat down to rest. Some new aches made themselves known to me as I relaxed. A man sat with an open newspaper, on a bench close by—my tail. He smiled and nodded. I ignored him.

On occasion he peered over the top of the newspaper at me and every passerby, to see if I made eye contact with anyone. After five minutes a sudden tiredness overtook my body and my chin dropped onto my chest. The uninitiated saw all the signs of a quick snooze on display. Although tired, my intentions didn't include a nap but rather to create the impression. A voice whispered from the vegetation behind me. I squinted through one, half shut eyelid to check on the tail and stretched my audible range to the limit.

"Eer, Guv! Don tern round. Tis me, Patch."

"I'm listening," I whispered.

"I fig'erd you might av told em bout me 'ence why's I'm in 'idin. Ah also let Mister Vermeulen know wot's been 'appenin."

"That's very intuitive of you, Patch. Do you have the little book?"

"Ah—yes. Tis'n interestin lil book, t'is."

"What's it contain?" For the benefit of my tail I followed my words with a gargantuan yawn.

"I thinks tis payments made to parlymentrary 'ficials, Guvner."

"Payments for what?"

"I'm not shoor but'm lookin inta it."

"Well, Wilcox is plenty worried about it—enough to threaten the welfare of my sister-in-law back home if you do not return the book."

"We'll ave ta figa somting out then, Guv."

"Can you contact Vermeulen and let him know my sister-in-law is in danger?—perhaps he can organize her safety."

"I'll doo 'at, Guv. Weese need ta foind anudder place to 'old talks."

"Where do you suggest?" I now became adept at talking like a ventriloquist with one eye shut and the other half open.

"Notta worry, Guv. I'll funds yer tomorra—maybe in tha street or a shop. Jes do wot yer normally do."

"Okay—and Patch?"

"Guvner?"

"Be careful."

A quick glance at my tail showed his continued interest in the daily news.

I heard the rustle of leaves, followed by a palpable silence.

∞∞

TWENTY-FIVE

If you are not living on the edge you are taking up too much room. —Jayne Howard.

My tail made no effort to hide his mission on the short walk back to the Horse's Head. He might have well come up alongside for a chat. The streetlights cast eerie shadows across the road as I hurried along. At the gates of the boarding house, another bloodhound took over and I assumed him to be the night-shift; not an envious job, outside in the cool night air—to stay awake and keep watch on my bedroom door.

Not tired enough to fall asleep my mind searched over the few options open to me. Contact with the police would be risky due to my break-in at the company's offices. I could try to leave London—but Wilcox, onto my every move, might have me beaten up again. There seemed to be no way out of the mess, unless I could arrange some leverage. An idea came to me—an unexpected revelation—Wilcox needed the book to avoid swift termination of his career as a politician. Possession of the sensitive information gave us the upper hand. Why did I not see this before?

I jumped out of bed and started to pace around the room. I could use the book to barter my freedom. Wilcox and King, by means of the contract held the deed to my farm and the mineral rights plus a potential future fortune, if the corundum business took off. To trade the book for the contract opened the door for me to clear away my indebtedness to the company. The thought took hold and I laughed aloud. Not my contract alone, but all the others in King's drawer. Wilcox would be forced to hand over all the files to me in exchange for the book. I didn't care what skullduggery he and the other members of parliament got up to. There appeared to be far more corruption in government than I could ever expose, but if my gambit proved successful all the faceless people caught in the company's clutches, received the reprieve they deserved—and their lives saved from ruin. A future circumstance might force Wilcox and King to reveal their heinous crimes.

Satisfied with the plan I climbed back into bed and fell into a fitful sleep.

*

After breakfast I wandered down some lanes, off the main street in the commercial area, to seek out small shops of interest. The bank, also on my list of things to do, required a visit—I needed cash to pay for the accommodation. After drawing funds I continued to walk down the busy street and found a small, corner bookstore, cozy enough for a good read. My tail entered in after me and made out to be interested in some magazines, while I scanned the shelves for literature. A few minutes later an older woman entered and stood behind me. She lifted a book off the opposite shelf and whispered out the side of her mouth.

"Patch sed ta tell ya ees in yer room 'idin in the cubbord."

My answer came without hesitation. "Thank you."

The old lady left and I decided to visit several other shops to complete the morning's foray. Once back at the Horse's Head and before I headed for my room, a quick visit to the John became necessary. I now suspected Patch to be in league with the old reception clerk—how else could entrance be gained to my room? I entered and locked the door, conscious of my tail who parked outside, in the corridor. The room appeared empty so I sat down on the bed to wait.

A voice came from the cupboard. "Ellow, Guvner. Don get up—I 'ave sum more noos bout the contents of th'book."

"I'm listening," I said.

Patch launched into a story of bribery and corruption which involved government officials and members of the police force. For Wilcox, this information in the wrong hands constituted a prison sentence—my plan if implemented required the utmost caution. The members of this bizarre cartel would stop at nothing to prevent the exposure of their dark secrets. To exploit the book any further, other than to gain possession of the contracts in respect to a potential arrangement with Wilcox, could invite my own demise—I'm not much of hero.

"I have a plan, Patch and I think it'll work. Is the book safe?"

An explanation of my strategy followed after his confirmation of the book's concealment.

"Will you go along with my plan? I know it sounds risky."

"I'm wif yer, Guvner. I don'care wot 'appens to 'ees blokes, long's I gets me payment."

At least I now knew where his allegiances lay— in the payment for services rendered. Vermeulen must have offered him a fair sum to help me.

"I think Wilcox will do as I ask. Sacrificing King's extortion racket in prevention of his entire world collapsing is a small price to pay. I'm going to make the offer and we'll see what he does."

"Suits me, Guv."

"Can we meet in the same way tomorrow? I should know my fate by then."

S'fine wit me, Guv. Go out fer yer walk and comes back jes like taday. I'll be a'waitin."

I left the room and made the short trip down the corridor to the dining hall. The tail, slouched against the opposite wall, straightened up and followed.

*

Wilcox sat on his throne and eyed me with suspicion. "You want to make a deal with me? What makes you think we're doing business, Satherwaite?"

In an attempt to hide fear I braced myself to answer the question. Mr. Ex appeared different today—agitated.

 "I figured you to be a wise man, Mr. Wilcox. You know what's at stake if the information in the book is leaked to the wrong people—people who are not in your pocket."

He glared at me with impersonal eyes and I feared my charade of bravado might be detected. "I'm listening," he said.

The tightness in my chest relaxed. "I am proposing to give the book back to you on one condition. My accomplice has it secured and so far, the only person to see its contents is him. He's an uncomplicated fellow, who doesn't really understand what's at stake here."

"And you are proposing?"

I took a deep breath. "I'm proposing you hand over all the files containing contracts like mine—all those documents in King's office—to me."

"For you to do what?"

"For me to destroy them and set those poor people free. You can use the company for whatever other purpose you want after that."

Silence reigned for a short period while Wilcox contemplated my answer.

"And you'll return the book to me, unseen by anyone else but your friend?"

"Yes. Once the book is back in your hands there's no proof of the things you are involved with. I don't give a hoot about you and your corrupt bunch of parliamentarians, Wilcox—I just hate to see the little people get hurt—people like me and those others in King's files."

Wilcox lifted his chin and gazed up at the ceiling, lost in contemplation.

"It seems like an equitable deal to me, Satherwaite. I admire your balls," he said. "How do you propose we make this exchange?"

"Milner Park—it's on Albert Street. It has an open grass lawn with cover at both ends. You come with the files and start from the South end—I'll bring the book and start from the North. We'll both move over the lawn towards each other and meet in the middle. The files and book will pass hands with an opportunity for each to check our acquisitions. We return to our respective ends of the park. No concealed weapons and no tails; no setups or traps."

Wilcox considered the plan. "When?"

"Tomorrow at midday."

Another short silence followed.

"I'll see you there, Satherwaite."

I nodded and turned to leave. Pig-eyes and Bob stood expressionless, one on each side of the door, but made no move to prevent my departure.

I passed through the building's exit and onto the street to feel the warm rays of sunshine caress my face. No one followed me. The tail stood at the steps and stared after me as if held back by an invisible hand, like a tethered terrier. The closer I got to the Horse's Head, the lesser my stress level.

One factor remained—Wilcox might be tempted to cheat. I thought it may be expedient to provide a backup. I'd rather err on the side of caution than blind trust. I couldn't believe my luck—one week in London and the achievement of my goal well on the way to completion. This suited me fine. Thoughts of South Africa flourished again but two steps remained after the completion of the deal with Wilcox—a visit to my mother in Margate and the arrangement of my passage home.

The sanctity of my room generated a strong notion of freedom and the sight of my bed prompted a nap. A while later I woke with a start to an unfamiliar noise. It sounded like a pebble, thrown against the window-pane.

∞∞

TWENTY-SIX.

Nothing succeeds like success. —unknown.

I jumped off the bed and went to the window. The late afternoon light suggested a longer nap than intended and a quick glance through the window revealed nothing of any interest.

A peek outside the door revealed little to get excited about. Now awake, I slipped my shoes on for a visit to the john and started my walk down the corridor when a voice whispered to me from out of the midst of a group of large Cornish-health plants in the adjacent garden.

"Ova'eer, Guv! Tis me, Patch."

A bench situated against the wall caught my attention and I sat down, opposite the plants. Patch could not know at this point the tails no longer presented a problem, however I couldn't be sure, so it seemed a good cautionary measure to take.

"I have spoken to Wilcox. He went along with the plan."

"Unky-dorry," chortled Patch. "Tomorrah as planned?"

"Bring the book and meet me in the bushy area in the north end of the park."

"Right-on, Guvner."

"We also need to have the backup as discussed."

"Twill be done, Guv."

I stood and continued on my way to the john. Later after dinner, I sat on the bed and tried to think of any additional problems we might face, but no tenuous situations came to mind. Robert King's reaction to his boss's deal with me might, on a second thought, be a legitimate concern. I expected no stoic dignity from the likes of King—vigilance throughout the transaction, would be paramount. To be safe my plan placed us at the north-end of the Park, amongst the larger bush and scrub at the verge, where flower-garden and lawn met. We planned to be there well ahead of time to eliminate the possibility of an ambush, before the transaction got underway.

I couldn't discount the fact King might take matters into his own hands in an attempt to turn the tables on me. He stood to lose a great deal of his ill-gotten gains through the loss of the contracts. I did not recall any copies in conjunction with the original document and assumed time constraints negated the practice of duplication—all the better for the successful conclusion of my plan.

The next day, after breakfast, I caught a taxi to Milner Park. In the North end, amongst the bushes I found Patch Foster and another individual.

"This 'ere is Burt, Guvner—an ol' frend o' mine."

I greeted Burt with a nod. His scruffiness complimented Patch's and apart from the eye-patch they could have been twins. Burt clutched an old army rifle, a Lee Metford with a makeshift scope and I guessed he might have seen some action in the war.

"Are we ready? Have you noticed anything out of the ordinary?"

"Nuffing, Guv. Awls quiet."

I glanced at my pocket watch—an hour to go. We waited and peered through the bushes across the grass lawn at the South end, for a glimpse of Wilcox and whoever he might have in accompaniment. At twelve I stepped out onto the lawn and waited, with black book in hand.

No movement disturbed the bushes on the far end. I waited a few more minutes before the bushes parted and a figure, dressed in an overcoat, stepped out to face me—Wilcox.

My walk toward him held as straight a line as possible. The knowledge of my two companions, hidden in the brush behind me, brought comfort and I hoped Burt possessed the courage to perform the allotted task, if required.

Wilcox and I arrived at the midpoint to stare at each other with a measure of detachment. We glanced around, ready for any sudden change in the stand-off and proceeded to exchange packages. Neither of us spoke in the process. I opened the South African file to check for my contract. The bright sunlight reflected off the paper and I needed to narrow my eye-lids to see the signature. Wilcox opened the black book and sifted through a few pages and closed it again. Both satisfied with what we saw we turned with simultaneous precision, like soldiers involved in a drill and marched off to the safety of our respective territories.

My labored breath eased with every step but I admit to being terrified throughout the entire exchange. The files in my arms represented the end of much misery, however, there remained one necessary action—to burn them, and I looked forward to the small bonfire. Back at the North end, amongst the first line of trees, a quick glance around for my colleagues followed. Patch appeared through a group of tall plants and slouched up to me with a lop-sided grin.

"Good stuff, Guvner. No trubble, then?"

I smiled and presented the files which he took from me.

A rustle amongst the bushes caught my attention and I thought it might be Burt but instead a stranger pushed his way through the scrub.

"Those files belong to us."

I did a double-take. So near and yet so far but I can't say we never expected to have trouble. The man held a service revolver, pointed at Patch's head. Another figure pushed past the stranger to survey us with beady eyes—Robert King.

He glared at me with malevolence and a cruel smile appeared on his lips. "Did you honestly think I would allow you to get away with something like this?"

"Wilcox and I had a deal, King."

"Wilcox is a spineless coward at times—All that really interests him is the damn book. I'm taking over from here."

With the sudden intrusion of King I forgot all about Burt. The distinct click of a rifle bolt sounded from behind the trunk of a tree and in its shadow the barrel of the Lee Metford became visible.

"Drop the revolver, Mister!"

King looked a picture of surprise. He didn't turn around but I could see his eyes swivel upwards in astonishment. The revolver fell to the ground with a thump. Burt to the rescue—my backup plan paid dividends after all.

"Do you have any matches, Patch," I asked.

He thrust a hand into his coat pocket and produced a box.

"I saw my contract amongst the bunch but just check it again."

Patch picked up the file and flipped through the contracts. He lifted one out and held it up for me to see. I squinted in the dappled light, caused by the overhead branches and confirmed the signature.

"Let's have a little bonfire," I said.

Patch grinned, struck the match on the side of the box and the files burned to ashes. Any future bid for King to extort more property and money ended right there.

"This ends your little scheme, King." I declared.

He gave me a murderous look. "This is not the end, Satherwaite. We will meet again."

"I certainly hope not," I said. "Goodbye, Robert."

Patch picked up the service revolver and we walked away from King and his companion.

∞∞

TWENTY-SEVEN

To accept defeat is nine-tenths of defeat itself.
—Francis Crawford.

I spent three days with my mother in Margate, Kent, where I grew up. So many memories flooded back from my childhood. The short stay brought much joy to my mum's heart but I was happy to leave when the time came. I thought it fortunate to have spent a mere two weeks in the achievement of my goal. My business in England counted as one of my worst life experiences but the success outweighed all the hardship.

My next aspiration, to become a citizen of my new home country, waxed strong as I stepped out onto the docks at Cape Town. I made a mental note to ask Vermeulen about it when I reached Kweetsa.

The journey by train tested my patience but ten days later I stepped out onto the station's platform to view the familiar vista of the hotel with its mountain backdrop. No one expected me to be home yet. I figured the short stay in London saved my benefactor a good deal of money, a debt I wanted to settle, when the Mine operation started up again. The need to meet this mystery person and offer my gratitude featured high on the list.

Without his generous offer of assistance I would still be a slave to the company. With the Corundum Mine back in operation there should be more than enough money available to pay back the loan, with interest. Maybe my benefactor might even consider coming in as a partner. We would need to find another company, a reputable one, who could manage the shipments and promote the mineral.

The short walk to the hotel took me a few minutes—old Cronje looked up from the reception desk.

"Where's Claire," I asked.

"Hello, Thomas. She's not here—visiting with her mother and children in Pietersburg."

I felt a little deflated. I thought about Claire on a regular basis and longed to see her again—much needed to be discussed.

"Can I borrow one of the horses to get to the farm?"

"Help yourself—I'm sure Claire won't mind."

"I'll leave my two suitcases here and send Polo to get them later," I said.

"As you wish."

I wanted to get home and have a decent wash. The ablution facilities on the train left much to be desired.

The ride out to the farm held a measure of excitement for me. I looked forward to the company of Letsatsi and Polo again, my two best friends in the whole world. I didn't see them as servants in the household—they constituted family.

The stupid dogs started to bay the moment I rode up to tether the horse to the rail in front of the verandah. Letsatsi ran out from the kitchen in response to the commotion, accompanied by a neigh from the stable. Dreamer, ears up straight and lips all a-quiver, trotted around the corner of the house—I guess he must have smelt me. Letsatsi beamed and curtsied, African style, as I walked up the steps.

"Morena, him home agen."

I gave her a hug but when I let go she clung to me and I waited for her emotions to ebb. When she let go of me her eyes gleamed with tears.

The Sotho peoples are a loving, uncomplicated nation who hold strong family values. I know my position as "Morena" on the farm elevated me above their considered stations in life but I saw them as my equals.

"Me go fech Polo."

She raced off along the path to the village and left me to check out extensions to the vegie garden on the side of the house, evidence of Polo's industrious efforts. Patches of cabbages and peas pushed up through the soil where dry, stony ground once ruled in conjunction with a multitude of weeds. It felt good to be home again.

Moments later Polo arrived, ecstatic to see me. To an outside observer, judged by the celebratory jubilation expressed, my absence may have appeared a great deal longer. We jabbered away; me with my pigeon Sotho, Polo and Letsatsi in their jumbled English. I told them my story with as much aplomb and excitement as Gulliver might have used on the return from his travels.

After an hour of talk Letsatsi pointed to the mantle-piece, above the fireplace, where an envelope sat.

My note to Olivia lay open on the coffee table. I took the envelope and saw my name in Olivia's neat hand.

"I need a strong cup of coffee please, Letsatsi."

She scurried off to the kitchen to make it while Polo hovered around the front door and waited for instructions.

"Take the buggy and go get my two suitcases from the hotel, Polo."

He dashed outside to fulfil my wish, happy to follow orders again.

I walked back out to the verandah and sat down to open Olivia's letter. The fragrance of cologne wafted up as the single page within, saw daylight.

"My dearest Thomas.

It has been awhile since we last spoke to each other. When you return from your travels you will no doubt need to see Mr. Vermeulen in Trichardt. Please consider a visit to my parent's farm. We need to talk.

I miss you terribly.
Your loving Olivia

In all honesty my thoughts of home, while in England, seldom centered on my tenuous relationship with Olivia. My sadness, coated with guilt vested itself in Claire's disappointment at my conduct plus my own low self-esteem, brought on by the loss of the farm. I'm not sure how I felt about Olivia anymore. My wife should be my closest family tie, but she seemed more like a distant relative. Thoughts about my marriage raised the lack of cohesiveness and the differences between our cultures. I read the letter again and a surge of guilt brought a lump to my throat. Did I love Olivia?

The question raged within me and brought an introspective gloom into the homestead. The doubt niggled at me and I attempted to dredge up the evidence which would cast a positive light on the strength of our relationship. Apart from the obvious physical appeal to my eye, she possessed the attributes of a kind and generous heart. But, on the darker side she displayed jealousy and stubbornness, traits that could easily ruin a marriage.

Letsatsi bumped my elbow with the cup of coffee and for a brief moment, confusion reigned until the coffee's delightful aroma brought me back to the present. The dogs came to settle near my chair —their large, Great Dane eyes searched mine as they lay with heads on paws, in hope of a tasty morsel.

A return to the question of my relationship with Olivia rekindled my need to brood. With vacant eyes I stared out into the Transvaal veld, oblivious of the sounds of the bird calls—my mind taken over by the battle of conflicted emotions and commitments.

Thoughts of her always raised visions of the many senseless arguments between us, about matters she knew little about. Whenever I felt down, the thought of Claire's presence nearby at the hotel, lifted my spirits. The contemplation of my relationship with her, in comparison with Olivia, held no negatives. I always found Claire to be level-headed, friendly and a well-balanced personality. Throughout the decade of marriage to Willy-John I had never known her to be jealous of anyone.

*

The next day, seated on Dreamer and engaged in a long-distance canter to Louis Trichardt, I considered the growth of the area since our arrival. The once, sleepy village now a medium-sized town, stretched out before me as we approached. The upgraded post office sported a parcel's department and a washroom, testimony to the growth generated by the travel of businessmen up to Rhodesia. New Industry and a shopping center monopolized the downtown section, supported by two suburbs, sprawled out on either side.

I made my way to Vermeulen's home with expectations of a long wait, until he could fit me into his schedule. Instead I found him at work among the fruit trees in the front garden.

"Afternoon Pieter," I greeted.

"Hello Thomas—one of my clients told me you arrived yesterday, welcome home. Come in and have a cup of tea."

With Dreamer tethered to one of the fruit trees I followed Vermeulen into the small home and sat down in the living room. He called to his mother to put a pot of tea on the stove and sat down opposite me.

"So, Patch told me you burned all the contracts?" He appeared less enthusiastic than expected.

"Yes, Patch and I did a jig around the fire. I would really like to conclude the business of the farm. Please tell me who my benefactor is so I can make a plan to pay my respects and gratitude," I said.

Vermeulen looked up at the ceiling and I detected a reluctance to answer the question.

"I have some bad news, I'm afraid," he said.

I leaned forward in the chair. "Bad news?"

"The saga with the farm is not over."

His words stunned me into silence for a few seconds before I regained my tongue.

"What do you mean it's not over? I burned the contracts myself."

Vermeulen adjusted the spectacles on the bridge of his nose and looked uncomfortable.

"Mr. King still has your contract and as the new director of the CBF Company he will continue to push for the confiscation of your farm due to your contractual disobedience."

The wind disappeared out of my sails and for a moment I thought it to be a dream—a nightmare.

"Mr. King has lodged the original contract with the High Court in Pretoria. It can be viewed by legal counsel at any time," he said.

My mind raged back to the day King and I confronted each other at Milner Park. Patch pulled my contract out of its file and showed it to me before we burned it, together with the other contracts. Did my own eyes deceive me?

I could see the document in Patch's hand as he held it up to the light which filtered through the overhead tree branches—I saw my signature. Or did I see a forgery?

"I think I know what King did. He must have made a second copy of the contract and forged my signature. Now, when I think back to the day when

Wilcox and I met at Milner Park, the bright sunlight reflected off the document and I struggled to make out the signature. The same with the final confrontation between King and I, the dappled light under the trees made it difficult for me to see clearly."

Vermeulen shifted in his seat. "So you burned the copy and left him with the original—how devious of him."

My heart sank. The entire trip to England, with incurred expense, offered no further progress than the day before I left. Hopelessness drifted over me like a dark cloud and I slumped low into the chair.

"Mr. King's attorneys sent me a cable from Pretoria which I received yesterday. They intend to take action and suggest counter measures by your legal counsel."

I shrugged. "I can't afford legal counsel—I'll have to hand over my property and be done with it."

Vermeulen leaned forward in his chair. "You do have legal counsel, Tom. I took the liberty of sharing this news with your benefactor who agreed I should be employed to fight the case in court, on your behalf."

"This mystery person is still willing to help me?" I felt a sudden rush of hope.

"I'm to take up the case immediately and send King's attorneys a notification of contest. The first thing we need to do is to file a notice of inspection and take a train ride to Pretoria, to have a look at the contract."

Restraint cautioned my response. "But, Pieter. Are you sure you can do this?—you're only starting out in your career—have you done anything like this before?"

"Not really—but my professor has a prestigious friend in Pretoria who will help us. Professor Malan is well known in all the country's legal circles and has practiced law for the past thirty years."

"But surely his costs will be enormous—what will my benefactor say?"

"Your benefactor has agreed to pay all the legal costs."

Once again I dangled at the mercy of this mysterious person. My intrigue grew in leaps and bounds—why his interest in my life and business? How does one repay such a debt?

I looked at my pocket watch—one pm. "I need to get going, Pieter. I still want stop in at Olivia's farm on the way home."

"I will let you know when I'm ready to make the trip to Pretoria," he said.

∞∞

TWENTY-EIGHT

Don't run from your weakness, you will only give it strength. —Stephen Richards.

About three miles outside Trichardt, on the road back to Kweetsa I turned Dreamer onto a rough path, which led to the Potgieter's farm.

The trail meandered through fields and past cattle, with heads raised, to stare at us—up a steep slope of a kopje, where on top, the view opened up into a beautiful vista of the veld. I could see the farmhouse in a hamlet about four miles away and spurred Dreamer into a canter down the slope.

A half-hour later the Potgieter's Boerboel, Simba, greeted us with enthusiasm, and we trotted up to the stable. I tethered Dreamer and a short walk, brought me to the steps of the farmhouse verandah perched under an elaborate overhang, which encompassed the exterior perimeter of the entire house. Olivia sat with her mother in the shade of the overhang, a glass of lemonade in hand. When she saw me round the corner of the barn she jumped out of her chair and came at a run.

I felt a sudden excitement to see her again. She stared at me, with lips parted and a look of surprise at my presence.

"Hello Olivia," I stammered.

"Thomas!" she threw caution to the wind and leapt into my arms.

"Oh, Tom, I've missed you so much."

Mrs. Potgieter looked on in silence. I could see my presence brought little in the way of joy for her.

"I've missed you too, my love," I said.

"Come inside and tell me all about your trip to England. The last time I spoke to old Cronje you appeared to have been successful in your quest."

I nodded at Mrs. Potgieter who returned a stony acknowledgment. Olivia and I moved into the living room and sat down on the settee.

"Daddy's away in Pietersburg for two days," she said.

I felt instant relief. Old Mr. Potgieter and I didn't see eye to eye and I think the last problem he needed in his life was a potential reunion between his daughter and the 'rooi-nek,' who married her—this Afrikaans expression referred to the English soldier's sunburned neck and emphasized the general hostile atmosphere between the two groups since the war.

I told Olivia some of the details of the trip, but left out the incidents to do with Wilcox, pig-eyes and big, bad Bob. I told her about King's devious maneuver, how he managed to retain the farm's contract. She listened and made sympathetic sounds of appeasement every time I stressed my sorrows. In the end she seemed a little more distant than before I related the bad news and I wondered how she felt about our relationship. Did the potential loss of the farm make our marriage less viable?

"Are you coming back to the farm," I asked.

"I think we still have some talking to do, Thomas."

'We can't talk unless we spend time together."

She sighed and fidgeted with the buttons on her sleeve. "I know this might sound silly of me but I think you do owe me an apology."

"An apology for what?"

"For what you and Claire got up to at the hotel."

Now I knew the reason for Mrs. Potgieter's coolness. No doubt the news of my impropriety with my sister-in-law rested on the lips of all her friends and associates—my apparent adultery the cause of their shame, in the tight-knit, Trichardt social climate.

"Dominee said I should never have married an Englishmen. He said all Englishman are traitors and black-skin lovers."

I looked at her through narrow eye-lids. "And you just believe everything your Minister tells you?"

"I don't, Thomas. You know I love you but your actions have caused a scandal in the community and I've been shamed because of it. My friends don't want to speak to me anymore."

"But nothing happened between Claire and me. I got drunk because I was upset at you leaving the way you did. She helped me to bed because I could hardly stand up and I slept in a store room, for Christ's sake."

My voice increased in volume.

"Shhhhh Thomas," she cautioned. "Mother will hear your words."

"I don't give a hoot about what your mother thinks—she hated me from the start." My anger, now kindled, knew no bounds.

"I think you had better go, Tom. You are angry at me and I'm not to blame."

"I'm, not angry at you," I said. I felt bad about my outburst. "I just feel unfairly judged."

I stood and took her hand. "Look, Olivia. I am going home now. If you want to join me at Kweetsa, you're welcome. It is your home and it's where you belong—not here in this cesspool of discrimination."

I turned and stomped passed Mrs. Potgieter. Her solemn glare followed in my wake as I hastened to the stable.

A short while later Dreamer cantered up a steep bank, onto the road between Trichardt and Kweetsa. Darkness filtered down through the trees and the horse took off for home at a gallop. He didn't let up until the hotel lights came into view and I slowed him down on the approach with the intention of a stop at the saloon. I needed a drink.

Two hours later old Cronje sidled up to me. "Pub's closing now, Thomas. You should make your way home."

When I moved my head the room began to spin and I fell off the stool onto the floor.

Old Cronje sighed in resignation. "What are we going to do with you, Thomas."

*

Vermeulen and I stared out of the train window at the bushveld, which passed in slow-motion before our eyes. With my mind full of the upcoming legal battle I'm not sure I saw anything at all during the trip.

The appointment of Professor Malan as the Barrister to present my case, took place in Pretoria, the administrative capital of the new Union of South Africa. The High Court of the Northern Transvaal would hear the case. Judges from the magisterial Districts presided over all cases with an estimated value below a thousand pounds sterling. Our case represented an amount far in excess of this figure. The other reason for the High Court's involvement rested in the Plaintiff's foreign status— an English company in business with

South African commerce by means of a special license, granted by the Government and the Chamber of Mines. The third reason centered on the involvement of a state department in conjunction with the Chamber, which required the presence of a jury.

The train took two days to reach Pretoria. Both Vermeulen and I, worn out from the journey, decided to register at our hotel first and get some rest.

The Sandspruit hotel near the law-courts close to Church Square, offered good accommodation; we each took rooms with a vista of Church Street, the busiest of all Pretoria's roads. I made a note to visit the site of the Union Buildings, the construction of which started in 1910—one of the hotel patrons felt it a sight to behold.

The next day, after breakfast, we walked to the Law Courts and enquired at the archives to view the contract. The clerk in attendance asked us to wait while he retrieved the document, which he placed on a wooden board under a sheet of glass. No one could touch the document until after the judges verdict, hence the precautions. Vermeulen studied it with the careful appreciation of a jewel merchant and made some notes in a small book, drawn from the breast-pocket of his coat. I gave it the quick once-over and confirmed it to be the original.

We thanked the clerk and left.

"Where are we meeting Professor Malan?" I asked.

"He will be waiting at Pretoria Station by the statue."

"The statue of whom," I asked.

"Paul Kruger, the military leader of the Boers and President of the old South African Republic."

"I finally get to meet the old beggar," I said. "I fought against his army at the Modder River."

Vermeulen smiled. "And you nearly lost your shirt."

He hailed a taxi as we exited the law court building to endure the bumpy ride to the railway station.

"It doesn't look the same as it did yesterday when we arrived," I said.

"Because we are at a different entrance."

We walked toward the statue and I noticed an old man on a bench close by. Vermeulen walked up to him and doffed his hat. "Professor Malan?"

The old man stood with the assistance of a cane and stuck out his hand. "In person—at your service."

The two men went off at a tangent in Afrikaans, a language despite all my years in the country, I could not get a handle on. I always felt uncomfortable in the presence of the Afrikaners because they represented the conquered foe—always felt a subtle hostility—a silent judgement passed, for the annexation of their country.

Vermeulen never gave me the impression, though. But now, in league with one of his countrymen, it may be different. We would have to see.

The old professor seemed friendly enough and I soon got to like him. We spent the rest of the day ensconced in law-talk over coffee in a corner café and by five pm I became quite bored with the issue. They knew of no similar case in the history of our legal system—much of what they said bordered on conjecture and precedence but they appeared to understand the possible outcomes. The old man took copious notes about the mineral rights and the times of the company's intervention on the scene. He wanted to know where Robert King came from and how I came to know him before the business approach.

At 5:15 pm we parted ways and Professor Malan hurried off to do some research into the agreement between the company and the Chamber of Mines.

It meant progress to Vermeulen, even if most of the discussion about the law went over my head. We retired to our rooms after dinner and on the next day, left Pretoria for Kweetsa. I hoped to see Claire at the hotel—I felt a strong desire for her company .

∞∞

TWENTY-NINE

The greatest pain that comes from love, is loving someone you can never have. —unknown

Two days later Polo came to me with a problem.

"Gkomo is missing, Morena."

He gesticulated toward the kraal where our small herd of cattle slept at night. Every day a herder released the four milking-cows to graze in the alfalfa field close by the homestead and the twenty-five beef cattle grazed daily out on the open veld, under the herder's watchful eye. In the early morning arrival of the herder at the kraal, he discovered three milking-cows, one less than the official number. He swore to the presence of four regular 'milkers' the previous night and the prognosis came down to cattle theft.

No presence of wild animal entry could be detected which left one viable possibility—thievery.

"Check the village kraal, Polo." I said.

"Is not by village, Morena—is gone."

I scratched the stubble on my chin and peered into the distance.

"I will have to speak to the 'Mapolesa' and ask if any other cattle in the district are missing—we may have a stock-thief on our hands."

The local district police in Louis Trichardt often received reports of stolen cattle. I thought old Cronje, always with an ear for news, might have heard snippets from the locals. It warranted a trip to the hotel, later in the afternoon.

"In the meantime speak to the villagers. They may know something."

"Ee, Morena."

At three pm I saddled Dreamer and left for the hotel. Another motive instigated my visit—to see Claire. Letsatsi made mention of Claire's return from Pietersburg the night before and I looked forward to a chat with her.

The pub bustled with patrons and old Cronje busied himself with the supply of drinks to thirsty travelers, who all vied for his attention at the same time. The train from Pietersburg made a regular stop for one hour, to take on water and allow passengers to disembark for a quick pint at the hotel. The engineer always gave three short blasts, ten minutes before departure time and everyone would chug their drinks down, to make sure they did not miss their ride.

I looked around for Claire but didn't see her anywhere. Old Cronje caught my eye and grabbed a bottle of Brandy from below the counter to pour a tot, supplemented by a half-glass of soda water.

"Have you seen Claire?" I asked.

He handed the glass over. "She's back from Pietersburg—arrived last night."

"How is she?"

He shrugged. "You know Claire. Never talks about herself but did say she met a gentleman on the train who showed great interest in her."

A shockwave shot through my system. I never considered she might look for male company. "This man is here at the hotel?"

"I last saw them sitting out on the back verandah having a drink."

My cheeks flushed and thoughts of concern entered my head. These dispelled under consideration of her independence and spawned a sense of self-guilt. I thanked old Cronje and slunk over to the corner, the saga of the missing cow now forgotten, to flop down into a chair. A sudden jealousy, at the intrusion of another man into Claire's life, overtook me—my relationship with my sister-in-law required more critical introspection. Why would her relationship with another man bother me to such an extent?

Another factor in contention was my wife, Olivia—where did she feature in this mess? The emotion stimulated a thickness in my throat I could not explain and it became apparent that I too, suffered from the same malady as Olivia—jealousy. As poignant as the condition appeared to be, I still could not help myself from indulging the sentiment. I felt a deep sense of hurt and loss.

Three short blasts sounded from the station. All the pass-through traffic stood to down their drinks and made their way out of the hotel. Within a few minutes the saloon emptied of people. I walked to the door which led out to the back verandah, for a quick check on Claire and her admirer. I saw them stand, shake hands and exchange salutations. It appeared the man would soon be on his way. It didn't look too serious, which made me feel better. I waited for them to complete their farewells and stepped closer in an attempt to assess the fellow's status in life.

He appeared to be about forty years old and his suit, made from an expensive foreign clothe with debonair cut, fitted him well. He doffed his hat and held onto Claire's hand for much longer than I appreciated, before he stepped around her to make for the exit. He brushed past me on the way out and I got a good look at his face—tanned and handsome. His eyes made brief contact with mine as he pushed past me.

Claire spied me at the door. "Thomas—how nice to see you."

She came over to peck at my cheek. The fragrance of perfume supplemented by her soft lips against my skin, cast their own spell and distracted me from the subtle resentment I felt toward her admirer. The moment brought one reality home to me—I loved this woman.

"Hi, sister-in-law—I've missed you. I see you were entertaining a friend?"

"Mr. Desmond Halifax. We met some time ago, back in Pietersburg—a real gentleman. He seems quite taken with me."

I raised my eyebrows. "And what did you think of him, besides being a real gentleman?

"He's very handsome and quite the charmer. I like him."

Will he be dropping in to see you again?"

"Why all the questions, Thomas—are you jealous?"

I blushed. "No. Just curious."

She decided to change the subject. "Tell me about your trip to Pretoria."

"It was very uneventful—did you speak to Vermeulen before leaving for Pietersburg?" I asked.

She looked down at her hands. "No but old Cronje did. He told me King still has your contract and is going to take the farm."

We moved into the saloon and I ordered another drink. Claire declined and opted for a glass of water instead.

I remembered the incident of the stolen cow and voiced my concern to old Cronje when he brought the drinks over.

"I haven't heard anything, Thomas but old sergeant Steenkamp from Trichardt usually pops in here during the week. I'll remember to ask him when I see him."

Claire placed her elbows on the table and leaned closer to me. "So, you met the person who will be assisting Vermeulen in your case?"

"Professor Malan—seems a knowledgeable old cuss," I answered.

"And you looked at the contract? Was it the original?"

I concurred and we talked on about the merits of a judicial victory. A quick glance at my pocket watch revealed the lateness of the hour.

"I better get back to the farm."

"We'll need some more beef and venison for the butchery, Tom."

"I'll see to it tomorrow," I said.

Dreamer declined to canter in the dark so the trip back to the farm in the moonlight, took longer than usual. It gave me time to think about Claire's position. She deserved a man in her life and this Halifax fellow seemed a good person. So, why the hollow feeling in the pit of my stomach—I should be happy for her, but instead I felt sorry for myself.

My marriage to Olivia should represent my future but instead, my decision to enter into the relationship, appeared to characterize my lack of good judgment. Deep down inside a realization of the truth, with regard to my real feelings for Claire, prodded at my conscience and I felt a twinge of guilt.

The dogs, asleep on the verandah, woke up to raise their heads at my appearance and give a cursory thump of the tail as I passed by and headed for my bed.

The next morning old Pheko, hypnotized by the first rays of the sun crowed his usual salutation to the new day. After ablutions I retrieved my cigarettes and walked out onto the verandah for a quick smoke before breakfast. The sun peeked over the horizon as Letsatsi waddled down the path from the village in song; it all seemed so delightful and African. She waved and slipped around the back of the house to enter by the kitchen door.

The previous evening's events gave me much to think about. Might Mr. Halifax call on my sister-in-law again any time soon? How did I feel about her with another man and in love again? Time is deceptive; Willy-John's death, almost fifteen months ago, seemed like yesterday—God, I missed him.

The divide in my relationship with Olivia had grown into a wide chasm. I preferred to gain a clearer view of the real issues but all appeared to be in limbo because of the court case. The farm's mineral rights and the status this afforded me in the small community represented my sole security.

I blew a cloud of smoke up into the air to give vent to my frustrations. Nobody would understand how I felt—maybe Claire, but her mind entertained another of my immediate concerns—Mr. Halifax.

After breakfast I picked up the Mauser and walked off into the veld to follow a fresh trail of hooves. The buck sensed my presence and stayed on the move, always about a mile ahead which afforded no opportunities for a clear shot. After four hours I turned back in discouragement to head for home.

On my arrival, a horse tethered to the rail in front of the verandah caught my eye. One person in the district owned a palomino as big and beautiful as this one—Olivia. She sat on the verandah, with lemonade in hand and awaited my arrival. Her presence produced a sudden negative emotion in me. The thought of another argument did not bode well.

"Hi, Liv."

She smiled. "Hello, Thomas."

I trooped up the stairs and sat down in a chair next to her.

"Don't I even get a kiss?" she asked.

I stood and bent over her with awkwardness, to deliver a peck on the cheek. "Sorry, Liv—but I have a lot on my mind."

"We've been like two ships passing in the night," she said.

"In a stormy sea," I added.

She laughed. "I'm sorry if I upset you on your last visit. I have thought a lot about it and I believe what you said—about you and Claire, I mean."

My thoughts on the ride back from the hotel the previous evening, came back to haunt and threw me into flux, a state in which I did not want to dwell. I felt a measure of relief at the confession and the pendulum of my angst swung in her favor.

"I want to come home, Thomas."

"You sure?"

She started to cry and pulled out a handkerchief from her sleeve.

"I've been so miserable and my parents have been so mean about our relationship. I've missed you," she said.

I could not resist her tears any longer and knelt down with my arms around her shoulders.

"I have missed you too, sweetheart."

We kissed with some hesitancy at first but passion caught hold and we retired the bedroom.

∞∞

THIRTY

Parents wonder why the streams are bitter when they themselves have poisoned the fountain.
—*John Locke.*

A week later I heard from Vermeulen. He came out to the farm for a quick visit after business in the Kweetsa community.

"We finally have a date for the case to be heard, Tom."

"That's good news. When?"

"On the 24th of next month. I will be spending some time in Pretoria with Professor Malan to prepare for litigation."

"Do you need me to be there at all?"

"Not until the day of the trial. I have all the details necessary for setting up the defense."

Olivia came out onto the verandah and put her arms around my waist. "What are our chances, Pieter?"

"I think we have a fair chance at proving there was intent to extort, but it will depend on the judge."

"At least things are finally moving in the right direction," I said.

Vermeulen placed his coffee cup on the floor and stood to leave.

"I will keep you informed." He kissed Olive on the cheek and shook my hand. "Don't worry—everything will be okay."

We sat and watched him ride off down the path. A powerful sense of gratitude overcame me.

"We have so much to be thankful for," I said.

"Have you figured out who your benefactor might be, Thomas?"

"Not yet—he must be wealthy, though. My guess is there has to be an interest in the Corundum Mine. Why else would anyone want to help me at such risk?"

"I'm sure we'll find out sooner or later," she said.

"I hear war is brewing between several of the industrialized nations in Europe—Germany and Hungary appear to be squaring off against Russia, France and Britain."

"Will it affect us here?" she asked.

"Not really but it might be good for the corundum business."

"We can't even think about the Mine until the business with the farm is squared away. Do you think we have a chance, Thomas?"

I shrugged and stared out into the veld. "I don't know, my love. We'll have to see."

In the distance I could see Polo on his mount, ahead of the cattle. The herder loped along next to the cows with an occasional crack of the whip and a shrill whistle, to keep the beasts in line. Polo's pony kicked up puffs of dust as it cantered along, ahead of the herd, toward the kraal. He opened the kraal- gate, waited for the cattle to pass through, turned the horse and headed for the house. I could see by the stance in the saddle he wanted to discuss an important issue. We waited for him to dismount and tether up to the rail before I greeted him.

"Dumela, Polo. O phela jwang?"

"Ke teng, wena o kae, Morena."

To greet someone in this way conveyed the staples of life, goodness and security, which in reality are not always the case. We tend to create similar clichés in the English language.

"I see there is a problem, my friend."

"Ee, Morena. There is gkomo missing agen."

I looked at Olivia. "I really have to get to the bottom of this. It's the second cow missing in a week."

*

Olivia and I decided to pay the police station in Louis Trichardt a visit. The three hour ride went by without incident. Olivia's palomino, still young and strong, led old Dreamer in the gallop and at times, waited for us to catch up.

Sergeant Steenkamp, a large, rotund man with heavy jowls received us with cordial aplomb and we got down to the business at hand.

"In the last week I've lost two cows. They've disappeared without a trace and we are wondering if anyone else in the district is having a similar problem."

The sergeant answered with a thick Afrikaans accent.

"Agh man, Mr. Satherwaite. Two farmers, this side of the river are also complaining about cattles lost. We are only two peoples here at the station and it's difficult to track down the perpetrators."

"Do you think the thieves are local people?"

"It's hard to say with these Blacks. One moment they're crying about the farmers being too harsh on them and the next moment they're pinching everybody's stuff."

"Do you think the farmers are too hard on their workers, Sergeant?"

"It's not for me to say Mr. Satherwaite—but I'll tell you what—I'll be looking out for your cattles."

"Really?" I said.

Olivia kicked my ankle under the table. Sergeant Steenkamp didn't respond but turned around in his seat to pull out a piece of blank paper from a shelf.

"Please draw your branding mark on this paper and sign it. Also state where we can get hold of you if we find something."

I did as he asked and handed the paper back to him. My first impression of the community police force suffered dismal disappointment. I didn't have the time to do any investigation on my own and if another cow disappeared, a trip to a higher authority in Pietersburg might become necessary. Olivia gave me a look of disapproval as we bid the sergeant farewell—my remark, "We leave it now in your very capable hands," did not go down well.

These people coexisted with her and carried a certain acceptance of each other as part of a larger family. Every Afrikaans person appeared to be an uncle or an aunt, a brother or a sister and I never did understand how it worked. I will say this for them, however—a courteousness and affection existed between all members of the community; a politeness which covered a multitude of sins and imputed a respectability. The young always respected and obeyed the old, no matter what—it fascinated me.

We mounted up and rode out to the Potgieter's farm. Olivia wanted to retrieve certain items, much to my chagrin. If I never saw her mother or father again it would be too soon—a mutual emotion, I should imagine. I tried to get out of the visit with a suggestion regarding chores to be done, back at Kweetsa, but Olivia did not back down.

"We are here now, Thomas. There's no sense me making another trip just to do this."

What she said made sense of course but it went much against my grain.

We arrived at the old farm house where Mrs. Potgieter sat on the verandah with a glass of lemonade, as usual. She employed a multitude of servants to do all the work which left her free to read books, stitch the odd garment and quilt to her hearts content. Her reaction at the sight of the dreaded son-in-law brought a smile to my lips. She jumped up from her chair and shot inside to call her husband who must have come in from the fields for afternoon coffee. They both popped their heads out of the door to stare at the two of us as we rode up to the tether-rail.

Mrs. Potgieter sidled out onto the verandah and stood with her hands clasped behind her back to greet Olivia in the Afrikaans language. She ignored me, as though I never existed. I jumped down from Dreamer's back to assist my wife in her disembarkation, while her mother remained on the verandah and stood with arms folded. I sensed a distinct air of tension in her conduct and she made no attempt to disguise her dislike of me.

Olivia ran up the stairs and threw her arms around her mother while I tethered the horses. The two turned and walked into the house without a word and I realized this is what the future held for me. I waited like a stable hand with the horses and regretted my compliance in the visit. This would be the last time.

Mr. Potgieter appeared at the door and walked down the steps. He gave me a cursory nod as he passed by on his way to the barn. I gathered nobody wanted to talk to me so I climbed back onto

Dreamer and waited. A few minutes later mother and daughter reappeared, Olivia with some folded dresses in her arms. She proceeded to strap them in a bundle at the back of her saddle.

Not once did Mrs. Potgieter look up at me or acknowledge my presence. The afternoon sun hung low in the sky. The trees, on each side of the path, cast long shadows and so, I decided to hurry matters along.

"It's getting late, Olivia—we should get going."

Olivia and her mother glared at me. You might have thought my crime bordered on the murder of the innocent and my offense exceeded the limits of forgiveness—they considered me to be no more than a dumb Englishman. Without any comment they continued with their chat as though plenty of time still remained for the journey back to Kweet-sa. I waited until Mr. P came out of the barn to say farewell to his daughter at which time she mounted up onto the Palomino. They said a final farewell and we turned the horses for home—at no time did they acknowledge my presence other than the nod Mr. P gave when he walked to the barn.

We rode off in silence. Dreamer, now home-ward bound, picked up the pace without any instigation on my behalf.

∞∞

THIRTY-ONE

Drink moderately for drunkenness neither keeps a secret nor observes a promise. —Miguel de Cervantes Saavedra

Darkness fell like a final curtain. The horses slowed down to a trot in the gloom as they adjusted to night vision. The hotel came into view and the lights beckoned with the friendliness of a small-town vicar. I reigned Dreamer into the front area and tethered him to the rail as Olivia rode up alongside.

"Why are we stopping here, Thomas? I'm tired and need to get home."

"I need to talk to Claire. I'll just be a minute," I said.

I walked up the stairs to the entrance and passed by the reception but did not see my sister-in-law. Piano music from the saloon indicated where she could be found and my heart gave an extra beat of joy at the thought of her company. The strains of the day also suggested a quick drink while Olivia waited outside. It may seem an immature response to the day's pressures but anger at her parent's attitude still festered within.

Old Cronje stood at the bar counter and thumped along in tune with the piano while the other patrons clapped their appreciation of Claire's musical abilities. Few people sat at the tables, the rest crowded around Claire who in turn looked at one person in particular; a man who stood at her elbow—Mr. Desmond Halifax.

His presence took me by surprise and I stared at the two of them with an open mouth; he appeared to know the song well and sang with a strong voice. The two appeared to be quite engrossed in each other, with smiles and laughter, supported by lengthy eye contact. Old Cronje tapped me on the arm to draw my attention.

"Bloke sings well doesn't he?"

My stiff nod telegraphed a reluctant agreement.

"They look as though they are enjoying each other's company," I said.

"Drink?" He asked.

I shot a glance at Halifax. "Make it a triple."

Old Cronje shoved the glass into my hand. Without a thought I downed the drink in one shot, slammed the glass down onto the counter and turned to glare at the people around the piano.

"Another," I said.

"Are you sure, Thomas?"

I glared at him. "I'm sure."

Another triple passed through my lips. The alcohol, now with a compounded affect, filtered through to my senses with serious potential consequences. I didn't know why I felt the way I did but Claire and Mr. Debonair, sparked off a rage within me. The day's trauma with the police, Olivia's parents and now this side-show, pushed me to the edge of a place I did not want to be.

"Oh, God. Olivia's still waiting outside. I gotta go."

Old Cronje gave me a startled look and waved as I peeled away from the counter to walk with much unsteadiness toward the door. By the time the fresh outside air hit me my knees threatened to go on strike. With a huge effort to retain balance I pulled myself up onto Dreamer's back and flopped into the saddle like a sack of grain.

Olivia looked on without amusement.

"Letsh go," I slurred.

Dreamer knew all too well his master's condition—now almost a common occurrence for him. He turned with care and trotted off in the direction of the farm. Olivia followed on behind.

By the time we arrived at the house the cool-night air came to my aide. The dismount, short of a fiasco, left much to be desired as Dreamer stopped at the rail to allow me an undignified exit off his back. I hung onto the saddle, to support myself for a minute, while Olivia dismounted and tethered her horse—I stood still in an attempt to stop the world, which spun with aggressive intent. She sidled over to smell my breath.

"You've been drinking."

Caught with my pants down it sufficed to say I didn't answer.

"Did you talk to Claire?" she asked.

I shook my head.

"So, all you wanted was a drink?"

I nodded.

"Thomas—I don't understand you. If you wanted a drink you could have had it here with me."

"Forget it," I mumbled. "Letsh go to bed."

"We'll talk about this in the morning when you're sober," she snorted.

It took several minutes, with Olivia's assistance to get me up the verandah stairs and into the bedroom before she could return to unsaddle the horses and bed them for the night. I passed out and did not even wake when old Pheko crowed in the dawn.

*

My head hurt every time I moved it. The effects of the alcohol limited my ability to greet the new day with any enthusiasm. Letsatsi greeted me with a smile and placed a bowl of porridge on the table for my benefit but I looked at her with my red eyes and turned away.

"Morena, him dlink too mush."

I thanked her for the candid observation and wondered off to the verandah with a cup of strong black coffee in my shaky hand.

"Where's Madam Olivia?" I asked.

"She gon to hotel, Morena."

I cursed under my breath. I knew why she left before I woke up—ammunition for the interrogation to come; to shoot down whatever reason I gave for the previous night's behavior.

The result of any apology, never enough to quell suspicions, would result in further argument followed by a move back to her parent's farm. I lived in a clockwork universe where all issues happened with predictable regularity—and the worst part—all my fault.

My immature reaction to the sight of Claire and Mr. Stupendous in concert together now appeared ridiculous to me. But it could not be undone. This realization dawned on me like a firework display on a dark night—my attachment to my sister-in-law surpassed any mild family affection—I loved her.

My marriage to Olivia wobbled on the ledge of a cliff. How much longer could I keep this farce up? At the same time, Claire deserved much better than me—I am not a Willy-John and never will be.

The sound of a horse on the path brought me out of my morose state of mind. Olivia always rode straight up in the saddle as though she paddled a canoe—the signs of her particular mission unmistakable.

She jumped down from the palomino and stormed up the steps toward me. I thought of the war years, when Willy-J and I confronted a Boer military party—I could see the same determination on her face. It must run in the genes.

I waited for the onslaught, my head already a-throb with pain.

"Now I know why you wanted to stop at the hotel." she said. "You wanted to be with that bitch but instead you found her with someone else."

"You spoke to Cronje?"

"He told me all about your mood when you saw her and this other fellow, having some fun at the piano."

I looked down at my hands and remained silent.

"Don't be mad at me, Olivia. Your parents totally ignored me when we visited yesterday and it upset me, even before I got to the hotel."

"Don't talk to me about my parents, Thomas. I saw how you looked at them. You hate them with a passion."

"They hate me with much more passion and you didn't make things any better yesterday."

"And what about your sister-in-law? You are in love with her, aren't you?"

She spoke the truth and the gates of my defense opened wide. I could not deny it—it made me sick to my stomach to think of my own deceit in the matter. I did not have any words for Olivia.

"Your silence tells me I'm right—this marriage is over!"

She stormed past me into the house. I raised my body out of the chair to follow her but the bedroom door slammed; a signal of total disengagement from the conversation. Letsatsi looked on from the kitchen and rolled her eyes at me—she didn't like Olivia and her disapproval showed. At least I could count on the support of one ally.

I grabbed the Mauser. "We need venison for the larder."

Letsatsi looked on in dismay as I stormed out of the house.

∞∞

THIRTY-TWO

Tis better to have loved and lost than never to have loved at all. —Tennyson.

Later, I returned to the farmhouse. A small rietbuck, with lifeless eyes, hung like the collar of a long fur overcoat, around my shoulders. I approached the front door and the dogs, on one of their endless sleeps, raised large heads to make lethargic thumps of their tails, in acknowledgement of my presence.

I called out to Olivia as I entered the living room on my way to the kitchen. Silence greeted me. Letsatsi came in from the backyard and stood at the kitchen door.

"The mosadi is gone, Morena."

Her reference to "The 'woman' is gone," showed the contempt she felt for Olivia.

I nodded and dropped the reitbuck onto the kitchen table for her to deal with and stalked off to the bedroom.

"The mosadi, she take Koloi."

I knew this did not bode well for a relationship which teetered on the brink of extinction. The two-wheeled carriage afforded a greater capacity for the transport of Olivia's wares.   A quick glance around the bedroom and a foray into her cupboard proved my assumption to be correct.

I padded out to the verandah and sat down in my chair. This time the dogs didn't even register. Letsatsi, in consideration of my dilemma, brought a cup of hot coffee for me to drink while I sifted through the ruins of my marriage. Earlier in the day while out on the hunt, I decided to settle on a complete confession in regard to my emotional attachment to Claire. The motive for this admission rested in a bad conscience but with Olivia now gone, the resolve, to follow up on my decision turned into resentment, fueled by her swift judgement of me.

The time to man-up and accept responsibility for the marriage failure hit me head-on. Olivia and I doubted the veracity of our union. Our backgrounds and cultural divide could not overcome the differences we faced. I resented the discriminatory nature her family held against all black people and they hated the English because of the war. No one could make a go of a marriage under those circumstances.

Time for another drink. I saddled Dreamer and we trotted off to the hotel. Did Claire's Mr. Halifax stay the night? I determined to be civil to him if it killed me. Claire could decide whom she wanted and if she chose him, so be it. I wanted to make sure I didn't complicate matters further, in our already complex relationship.

The train to Pietersburg pulled into the station at the same time I rode up to tether Dreamer. The horse nudged my arm as I gazed across the field at the passengers on their way down the path toward the hotel. I thought of Halifax—would he leave when the trained pulled out in an hour? He must have stayed the night because the last train to Pietersburg left an hour before Olivia and I arrived on the previous evening.

In whose bed might he have slept? I shrugged off my negativity and stomped up the stairs into the reception. Claire looked up from the desk and greeted me.

"Hello, Thomas. I saw you last night but you didn't wait for me to finish up."

"I saw you were occupied so I decided to push on through to the farm." I said.

"Did I see Olivia waiting outside for you?"

"Yes, but I wanted to ask you about the needs for the butchery. Two cows have been stolen in the space of a week and our milk production has dropped."

"I'll check with Cronje—I think we might need at least another ten gallons. Are you not feeling well? You look a bit down."

My face always gave my emotional state away. It's difficult to hide emotions when you're the type who wears your heart on your sleeve.

"Olivia has left me. I think for good this time."

"Oh, Thomas—I'm so sorry—I didn't know you had marriage problems."

I blurted out the whole story about my visit to the parent's farm and the breakdown in our communications.

"I can't take the mood swings anymore. Her parents hate the sight of me and jealousy rules her life."

"Don't you think it's all caused by the pressure of possibly losing the farm?"

"I know I've been a bit off because of the court case story but dammit, Claire, I'm not that impossible to live with."

"Perhaps she doesn't understand the pressure you're under. Do you think it would help if I spoke to her?"

I shuddered to think of the consequences. "No—it's best left alone."

"Perhaps you should just give her a little time."

"I gave her a couple of weeks the last time she left but it didn't really help."

"What is she jealous of?"

The question caught me a little off guard. "Er—she's...actually jealous of you."

"Of me? Why me?"

"Because you and I have a much longer family relationship and I must admit, I prefer your company to hers."

Claire stared at me. "Probably not a good admission on your behalf."

"No—but It's a truthful one."

Our eyes locked for a long moment before she broke away and shook her head.

"Let's go 'and get a drink," she said. "I guess the night you got drunk and slept in the storeroom caused the trouble. It's your own fault, Thomas."

We moved from the reception into the saloon and old Cronje's son asked regarding our choice of drink.

"Is your dad not well again, Hennie?" asked Claire.

"He is very tired, Mrs. Satherwaite."

A thought struck me—if I ever married Claire she would not have to change her last name—it's an odd thought to cross one's mind.

We sat in the corner with our drinks and my self-consciousness heightened due to our earlier conversation. I sensed Claire's omniscience in the matter of my conflicted emotions and felt awkward about my lack of confidence.

"I guess your friend Mr. Halifax is still here?"

"Yes, he is. He stayed the night at the hotel and is busy packing his overnight case for departure to Pretoria. The train leaves in about twenty minutes."

"I should like to meet him," I said.

"You will, here he comes."

I turned to look toward the reception to see Desmond Halifax on his way across the floor to our table. The tall, slim frame and broad shoulders projected an urbane air of confidence. Due to the coolness of the evening, brought on by the autumn season, he wore a full length coat over his suit.

"Claire, Darling—I'm ready to take off," he said.

Surprised to hear the Canadian accent I leaned back in my chair to listen.

"It was good to see you again, Desmond. Will you pass this way again?"

"I most certainly will, my dear. I can't pass up an opportunity to spend a few moments with the most beautiful woman in the Northern Province."

Claire blushed and glanced at me. "I would like you to meet my brother-in-law, Thomas."

Halifax extended his hand and I shook it with the strongest grip I could muster.

"It's good to meet you, Tom. Claire has told me much about you and your late brother."

"Thank you, Desmond. It's good to meet you, too."

He smiled and made to leave. "Are you going to accompany me to the station, my dear?"

Claire pushed her chair back. "I'll see you onto the train."

A jealousy clawed at my gut as she took his arm and together they strolled out of the saloon—should have offered to accompany them. Desmond Halifax seemed a likable guy but his intrusion into our lives presented a complication—a distraction my sister-in-law and I could well do without.

Claire turned her head to catch my eye. "Good night, Thomas."

I waved and watched them pass through the reception to the front entrance. My mind churned with self-deprecation—should have jumped up and offered to go with them, or at least offered to wait for Claire until she returned. Damn!

Young Hennie caught my eye. "Another drink, Mr. Satherwaite?"

"Why not," I mumbled. On arrival at the hotel earlier my conviction, not to get drunk but to enjoy an evening with Claire, fell by the wayside. The main purpose no longer existed. The woman I loved and idolized appeared oblivious to my presence.

∞∞

THIRTY-THREE

If there were no bad people, there would be no good lawyers. —Charles Dickens.

Vermeulen met me at the hotel for the trip to Pretoria and the first court hearing.   A cable, which stated the Case number and legal tag, preceded the appointment:

First hearing of:
The CBF Company verses Mr. Thomas James Satherwaite.
At 11:00 am on 24th October, 1913.
The High Court of the Northern Transvaal, Pretoria.
Union of South Africa.

Vermeulen and Professor Malan would be engaged in my defense of the farm's mineral and property rights, against the plaintive Robert King of CBF.

Professor Malan's prognosis rested in previous observations of the particular Judge, whom he felt leaned toward local businesses in legal battles which involved entities from beyond the borders. The South African law system, as Vermeulen described, contained both elements of civil and common law but since the war the new Union of South Africa tended toward change. The High Court of Pretoria would see our case because it involved the claim of business rights overseen by the South African Chamber of Mines. I didn't understand a word of all the legal jargon but there is a reason why lawyers get involved in these disputes.

My South African residency qualified me to be represented on the same basis as a citizen so I might expect the judge's judicial scales to tilt in my direction. This did not, however, rule out the legality of the contract held by Robert King. My defense would rest on the pretext of a deliberate omission of important details on behalf of CBF Company, in an effort to grab the farm with its mineral rights.

Throughout the trip to Pretoria Vermeulen said little. My concern over his preoccupation with the purchase of a new toy, a motorized car, left me with some doubt as to his legal concentration.

We stayed at the same hotel in Pretoria and met with Malan on the night preceded by the first appearance, to discuss the merits of the defense's approach.

"King has nothing other than the contract to fight this case with. His company never put one hour's work into extracting the minerals and the promise of bridging finances was never met," said Vermeulen.

"We have to be careful in the way we present CBF, though—as an entity which extorts money out of the unsuspecting—I have tried to contact some of the victims but because the contracts were all burned by our friend here, we cannot claim loss of any property."

"Were any of the victims prepared to testify as to the company's claims on their properties?" I asked.

Malan scratched at a mole on his face. "Not one of them wanted to travel here for the case—they said CBF contacted them to let them know they were off the hook regarding their contracts."

"King deliberately did it. He knew they would be glad to evade the loss—also to wipe their hands of anything more to do with the company," said Vermeulen.

The evening wore on until I declared my need for sleep. The lawyers agreed and we called it a night.

The next morning at 11:00 am everyone gathered in the court house to face the judge and for the first time since my return from England I saw Robert King. He gave me a casual nod as he sat with his counsel and I suppressed a strong desire to get up and strangle him. The smirk on King's round, red face revealed his unbridled arrogance and I wanted to wipe it off with my fists but the deterrent of contempt prevented me.

The presiding official, Judge Bernard Breytenbach, called the court into session and the counsel
for the plaintiff stood to present his client's reasons for the litigation against me. When he finished, Vermeulen stood and presented a rebuttal
of the indictment and asked for the charge of "contract default" to be thrown out.

The judge listened with interest to my story
and how King made the initial approach. He also
listened to Robert King's version without comment. He made some notes in an open file, told
everyone to be seated and called on the clerk for
the trial's date to be set.

The clerk pulled out a clipboard with a host of
paperwork and scrutinized it with care. "The 5th of
December, Your Honor— with the presence of a
jury and in this same courtroom."

The judge banged his gavel on the sound
block to declare the hearing at an end.

I looked over at King as I stood to move out
from the counsel's table and caught him with an
ear inclined toward his lawyer, who whispered
some words to cause their amusement. They both
looked over at me and King shot me a disdainful
glance. Professor Malan took my arm and guided
me out of the courtroom.

"Don't allow yourself to fall for their cheap
shots and sneers," he said. "Let the law decide the
outcome."

"I think we made a good impression on the judge," said Vermeulen. We left for the hotel and ended up in the bar for the afternoon. The professor retired to his room at 4:30pm.

"Please tell me about my benefactor, Pieter," I pressed.

Hope of a loosened tongue induced, through the few drinks imbibed by my lawyer, encouraged me to badger him about the identity of my mysterious patron—the kind person who put up all the money for my trip to England and now the defense of my case.

"You know I cannot tell you anything yet, Tom. I'm under strict instructions to keep it a secret. If my client knows I have told you I will be fired."

I came up with more reasons why he should relent but he shot down each attempt. At 5:30 pm we went to the dining room for dinner and I drank a few more brandies. Due to a serious problem with coordination Vermeulen helped me to find the way to my room after the meal and I flopped onto the bed to dream of Claire and Desmond Halifax.

We left Pretoria the next morning and three days later arrived at Kweetsa where I walked to the stables to look for Dreamer. To my surprise Claire popped her head out from one of the cubicles. "Thomas—where on earth have you been?"

"I attended court—the first hearing of my case, with Vermeulen and Prof. Malan."

"Why didn't you tell me you were going—I've been worried out of my mind. I rode out to the farm and Letsatsi didn't know where you were. She said you went away for a few days—she's so protective of you."

I laughed. "I hope she doesn't put you in the same league as Olivia."

Claire put her arms around me and pecked my cheek. "I missed you, Tom."

Confusion reigned supreme. She dumped me the other night and now she tells me I am missed? I couldn't make it out but the thought gave me a tremendous amount of satisfaction. My heart lurched as her body pressed up against mine and the fragrance of perfume wafted up into my nostrils. The soft feel of her breasts against my chest sent the old libido into a tailspin and we stood there —the best moments of my year so far.

The dream dispelled like a puff of smoke, however, when she became self-conscious of our intimate position and the sudden movement of a certain member of my anatomy against her thigh.

"Don't do that to me again," she said.

My confusion must have showed.

"I mean, to go away and not let me know—you are, after all, family, Thomas."

I managed a self-conscious smile. "Well I'm glad you got that question out of the way."

My hopes plummeted again. I wanted to be more than family.

"Do you want to eat at the hotel tonight?" she asked.

"If it's an invite then I'd love to."

She grabbed my arm and we walked out of the stable toward the hotel steps. I placed my suitcase behind the reception counter and we moved into the saloon to the sight of old Cronje in remonstration with one of the black kitchen staff. Claire took over the problem and allowed Cronje to serve some other customers.

When she returned to the table she carried two drinks in her hand. I looked at her attractive face and short cut dark hair as she placed the glass before me. For a second our eyes met and somehow in the moment there seemed to be a sensual encounter, a promise of a closer relationship.

"So did Desmond get away safely on the night I last saw you?"

The question of where this man stood in the scheme of our complicated relationship, weighed on my mind like a sack filled with rocks.

Claire gazed into my eyes and took my hand. "Why do you ask, Tom?"

My face must have turned pink under the blush. I gazed back at her and bit my tongue. "I am interested to know what he means to you."

She strengthened her grip on my fingers and smiled.

"Are you jealous of him, Thomas?"

Again, I didn't know how to retain my composure.

"Maybe."

She let go of my hand. "Mr. Halifax not only has good-looks but he's also quite a lady's man. I know he is infatuated with me and keeps making suggestions we would be good together."

I bowed my head and asked, "Are you considering marrying him?"

"He hasn't popped the question yet—our association is more along business lines at the moment."

Hope fluttered into contention again. "Tell me about it."

∞∞

THIRTY-FOUR

The way to love anything is to realize that it might be lost. —G.K Chesterton.

Claire straightened up and folded her hands. Her beautiful, hazel eyes locked with mine as she began her story.

"I first met Desmond in Pietersburg while looking for new cosmetics in one of the downtown shops. The servers were all busy and I, being interested in one of the products stood by waiting to be helped, when this debonair gentleman came across the floor. He introduced himself and started to explain the history behind the product of my interest."

"Did you think he was making a pass at you," I asked.

She laughed. "No, not at the time but he is a very charming person. It turned out he pioneered many of the current cosmetics for women, plus the one in my hand. He offered to let me take it for free and try it out."

"So you agreed?"

"I used the product for three days and found it to be of exceptional quality so I returned and told him so. We met again on the train and he told me more about himself. He is a millionaire who owns ten brands of cosmetics and has factories in different parts of the world. He asked me what I did and I told him about the Kweetsa business community."

I shifted in my seat to get comfortable. "Did you tell him what happened with the farm?"

"Yes—he commended me for separating the businesses from the farm. He said I showed good, solid business sense."

I took a tentative sip. "I also believe you showed good sense. Just think if we both had run afoul of King."

She looked down at her hands. "Desmond said he wanted to invest in my businesses. I felt flattered."

"On what basis did he want to invest?"

"He came up with some good ideas to promote the area and even kick-start the beginnings of a village, with its own town hall. Will and I often talked about this prospect but we didn't have the money for such a venture."

I flinched. "I hope you didn't decide anything."

"Not yet—you know how cautious I am."

We sipped on our drinks for a while before I plucked up the courage to throw in my two pennies.

"I would love it for you and I to be partners again, Claire. If I can get the farm back and the corundum mining comes through, we could make a good fortune together."

She looked at me with sad eyes. "You don't have the farm back yet. You shouldn't count your chickens before they hatch."

"But if it did happen—would you consider it?"

Again she hesitated. "I don't know Thomas. I need to consider Desmond's offer as well. I can't talk about it now."

Three blasts shrieked out from the steam engine, ready for the next leg of its journey and I glanced at the saloon clock. "It's time I got going for home," I said.

"I took special care of Dreamer while you were away—I asked the stable hand to make sure he's saddled and waiting for you."

I took her hand in mine. "Please consider my offer, Claire. Don't make any hasty decisions about doing anything with Desmond."

"When is the court date for your case?" she asked.

"Give me to the 5th of December—I'd better go."

I pecked her on the cheek and left the saloon.

*

The midday sun reached its zenith in the sky as the hunt, which started at 6:30 am, came to end. A small duiker hung over my shoulders, the single prize after five hours of toil. The backend of the farmhouse appeared through the umbrella thorns and I could see old Pehko, like a lone sentinel on top of the coop, with an eye out for his entourage of hens.

I trooped into the kitchen through the backdoor and laid the buck on the table for Letsatsi. She gesticulated toward the front verandah to indicate the presence of a visitor. With the Mauser secure on its hooks above the fireplace I walked through to the verandah and found Vermeulen in one of the chairs with lemonade in hand.

"Afternoon Pieter. What brings you out to Kweetsa today?"

Vermeulen rose and shook my hand. "It's a bit of a sensitive matter, Tom. I am perhaps the bearer of bad news."

He reached down to his leather briefcase and extracted a wad of documents.

"What's this about?" I asked.

"Olivia is asking for a divorce," he said. "These papers are the summons for the action. She's not asking for anything from you so it will be an uncontested action or 'undefended,' as they say, providing you agree."

I felt shocked at the suddenness of the news and gazed at the documents with surprise.

"I've been meaning to make contact with her but the farm's case has occupied my time," I said.

Vermeulen looked on with sympathy. "There are only two reasons for a divorce under South African law—adultery and malicious desertion.

Olivia has said that she will accept the position as defendant and allow you as plaintiff, to sue for abandonment.

She believes that the circumstances of your relationship with her family, are irreconcilable and the differences in culture, to vast to bridge—it was a grave mistake, as she put it. You can take your time reading through the documents but basically if you sign the summons you are suing her for desertion. She will not defend the action and the case will be set down for a hearing in the High Court."

"Why do I have to sue her—can't she sue me?" I asked.

"She can't sue you because she is the one who has left the home."

"What happens if I refuse?"

Vermuelen shifted his position in the chair. "If you refuse then you will remain married to her and will not be able to legally marry anyone else? Is that what you want?"

I thought of my position. I could only hope that my relationship with Claire would blossom. It seemed to be my sole possibility of happiness in this life. I could not see reconciliation with Olivia's family becoming a reality.

"Will we have to appear in court?"

"Yes, for the hearing—if it's not contested there will be no need for excessive costs."

I felt as though I'd been punched in the belly. It's not as though I didn't expect action on the matter but to be slammed with divorce papers without any discussion seemed a bit much. My wife's apparent haste concerned me and in preference, I would like to have spoken to her about the situation before we embarked on such drastic action.

"I'll go through the documents and bring them to you in a day or two," I said.

"As I said, Thomas—take your time."

I thanked Vermeulen and he left.

So much water under the bridge in so short a space of time. My overwhelmed state of mind refused to compute. An emotion welled up through the flotsam of the divorce action—to my surprise, it felt like a cautious relief. I looked at the documents again and read about the constructs of my marital fate.

Later in the afternoon I decided to go for a walk to the village. Polo's absence made me wonder what he might be up to. His wife stood at the entrance of their mud-hut and curtsied as I approached.

"Dumela, Morena."

I answered in the traditional way and asked about her husband. Her face reflected youthfulness—she wore a blanket around the slim, but well-formed young body. Strapped on her back and wrapped in a shawl, a young baby with large, dark eyes, stared out at me.

"Polo, him go look for mashodu."

An urgent matter must have come up. His wife intimated her husband's mission involved a thief and might be dangerous.

"Gkomo?" I asked. The stolen cattle came to mind.

"Ee, Morena."

After a few more questions she divulged the time of his departure—5:30am in the morning. I couldn't understand why he decided to go off alone as we always investigated stock-related incidents together. No further information about his mission came to light so I thanked her and left, after she promised to send word when he returned.

Back at the farmhouse I sat down on the verandah to enjoy a cigarette and coffee. My mind returned to Claire's relationship with Desmond Halifax and for the first time a determination rose in my heart, to make every effort to win her over. I saw Halifax as a rich opportunist who would take advantage of the woman I loved—an unacceptable state of affairs. Favorable sentiments for Olivia hung in the balance. Her decision to divorce revealed a dearth of genuine love for me and I imagined a heavy parental influence played a huge part in her decision.

Claire on the other hand suffered vulnerability. Her need for a partner in life to provide stability and love, to help with the businesses and be a protector of her interests, might drive her into the arms of one such as Halifax. I couldn't allow it to happen. To make a better foundation for a relationship with her I needed to man-up and become the person she would choose– restraint at the over-indulgence of liquor headed the list of my new-found resolutions. No woman wanted a man whose horse stood between him and significant injury every time they rode back from the hotel at night–a man, who in his drunken state could not focus enough to guide his own steed.

I sat at the kitchen table and reread the divorce requirements by the light of the lantern, gathered my writing equipment together and signed on the dotted line. With a sense of finality I folded the documents and placed them in the envelope for delivery on the following day.

Back on the verandah I indulged a final cigarette before bed and reflected on my situation. With my head at rest against the back of the chair I thought about Claire. In my mind's eye I could see her slim, curvaceous body standing on the top of Kweetsa hill—reminiscent of a day in the past, when Willy-John and I took the afternoon to walk with her to the summit. She wanted to see the view.

As she stood in awe of the scenery below us, the wind caught her dress and before she could bring it under control, it fluttered high around her waist. That mental picture stayed with me and although I had no designs on her at the time, as a bachelor the image often consumed me.

I remembered her hair, blowing around her face in a swirl and a glimpse of the close-fit underwear, revealing milky-white high thighs. This tantalizing sight created a path along which my mind never ceased to wander and I realized, subconsciously, I wanted her more than anything in the world.

My cigarette, smoked to the butt, singed my fingers—time for a quick wash and then, bed. Another lonely night lay ahead but on the morrow I looked forward to a trip to Louis Trichardt, and a visit with Claire at the hotel. Armed with this consolation, I blew out the lantern's flame and fell asleep.

That night I dreamed. Dreams are often fuzzy in character and are sometimes vague in their interpretation—this particular dream remains one of the most vivid I have ever had and one I wished, at the time, would never end. We always wonder why we dream about certain people but when I awoke, the reason for this one, appeared plain to me.

In my dream I walked on fine sand, beside a beautiful stream. The sun filtered through the branches of full, lush trees; birds warbled beautiful avian songs and the warm air suggested the slightest hint of a breeze on my naked skin. My nostrils filled with the fragrance of exotic plants, to bring a euphoric feeling of nostalgia. I became conscious of a figure beside me...my soul filled with happiness, pushing away my loneliness—sensual vibrations emanated from the loving heart of the angel standing next to me. I didn't need to look at her ethereal face. My heart and body knew it was Claire.

She looked up at me with her beautiful dark-brown, soulful eyes and smiled. She wore a flowing cotton sundress, as white and pure as the clouds floating in soft puffs—an overwhelming need, to have her with me, have her close, almost took me to my knees. My fingers longed to trace her soft skin. My body screamed to feel her heart beat in sync with mine, to have her under me as she cried out her passion. I stopped to draw her closer but she kept on walking. A backward glance revealed a hunger as strong as mine burning in her eyes. She stopped and raised her beautiful face to the filtered light. She shined like a million suns, all heating my body to a boiling point. I longed to trace her delicate neck with my lips, to taste her essence. Dear God, my lungs refused to take in air, in such a state of awe at the image before me.

In frustration, I reached out my hands to convey the ache in my heart, to hold her. She came to me. A swirling mist rose from the stream and engulfed us. With the sight of her lost my remaining senses screamed out for greater efficacy—then I felt the softness of her skin and the warmth of her body, pressed close against my own. Our lips met in a long, passionate kiss. I slid my hand over her shoulder, to slip the dress's strap, along the silky skin and allowed my thumb to lead over her full breast. She shuddered and a moan escaped her throat.

Her fingers brushed along my chest, sending tingles rushing to my loins. This woman made me crazy with a single touch. My heart wanted to give her everything, my body desired to make her forget any other man ever existed. A hot hand wrapped my manhood, almost undoing me right then. Her touch was pain and pleasure, torture and ecstasy.

In my dream, my eyes opened to see her loving face, her lithe body, under mine. My breath stopped as I slid into her burning core. Oh God, so hot, so right. Yes, right. Our souls belong as one, this vision of heaven with a lost, lonely wanderer longing for her love—then came the worst type of ending to a dream; old Pheko's crowing in of the first light.

The dream imploded. I felt a moment of brief desecration as the truth dawned, to leave me bereft of the love I carried with such intensity in my heart.

How would I live without her?

∞∞

THIRTY-FIVE

Law is order and good law is good order.
—Aristotle.

Polo stood on the verandah with hands in the air, accompanied by a loud verbal reproduction of his discoveries. For me, two days of work in the garden followed the uneventful visit to Trichardt for delivery of the divorce documents. Claire's busy schedule with the businesses prevented me from the intended visit but the determination still remained to showcase the new 'me' at the earliest opportunity.

My scheme to present this entailed an approach to old Cronje to set up a romantic dinner for the two of us one night, outside on the saloon's back verandah, before the date of the court case. I wanted to show Claire I felt optimistic about the future, whatever it held.

I sat in my chair while Polo went off on his tirade about the boyfriend of a village girl—a man who did not live in the village but on a neighboring farm. It appears this man, aided by two of his cronies, took our two cows to slaughter them and sell off the meat. Polo picked up this information from the young children at one of the kraals and followed up on it on the day of my visit to the village. He confronted the girlfriend and threatened to tell her father—she confessed.

I asked about the final outcome of his investigation.

"Mashodu, hims not see me follow, Morena. I see the kraal for him. We set trap."

"When are they going to steal another gkomo," I asked.

"Girlfriend for mashodu say tonight, Morena."

"From our kraal?"

"Ee, Morena."

*

Bushveld nights are almost as bright as a dull day. The full moon, plus the combined light of a billion stars in the Milky Way, provided enough illumination to see for miles.

Polo and I, together with two of the village elders, sat under a buffalo-thorn about thirty yards from the cattle kraal. The sounds and scents of the veld floated on the light breeze as we waited, our eyes riveted on the pathway to the gate. I gave the stock of the Mauser a gentle rub with the inside of my hand—it generated a unique sense of security. Polo held two stout, traditional sticks as did each of the elders. Doubtful of the thieves' armed capability, or possession of dangerous weapons other than traditional sticks, I felt we would have the upper hand.

After two hours I began to feel impatient and wondered if our source of intelligence might have got the wrong evening but a sound of footsteps, first picked up by Polo, got our attention. In the gloom we could see two men in a crouch with their sticks in hand. The direction of their stealthy advance confirmed the destination—the cattle kraal. They stopped at the gate and heads swiveled in all directions for detection of any danger—we held our collective breath.

The lead man worked on the unlocked chain, at the gate and threw it on the ground. The gate swung open with a slight squeak of rusty hinges and they slipped into the kraal like ghosts. Once closed, the gate cut off any escape from the confines of the Kraal. We crept up to the entrance like four stealthy leopards and closed the gate.

The thieves' selection, a beef cow, made a startled grunt as one of them placed a rope around its neck and turned toward the exit. When they saw the four of us in the gloom they let out cries of fear and fell to the ground with hands raised in the air. The sticks reigned down with heavy blows on every part of their anatomy. Polo swore a stream of Sotho expletives and the two elders whooped war-cries.

The two thieves, their cries for clemency subdued to whimpers, lay on the ground in an attempt to protect the more delicate areas of their bodies—so ended the saga of stolen cattle. I decided not to press charges against the two teenage boys. Polo and the elders beat them to within an inch of serious injury and we determined legal retribution would ruin their futures. The elders agreed to sought it out with the two boy's parents and extract some form of compensation from them.

We let them go after a lengthy interrogation and called it a productive night.

*

The 5th of December arrived without fanfare. Vermeulen and I made our way from the hotel to the station. The night before, Claire and I spent two hours of enjoyable discussion over a meal arranged by old Cronje and paid for by me. My conduct bordered on the sublime. Limited to one drink for the duration of the evening, I steered the conversation down positive avenues. At the end of the evening Claire commended my conduct and said she knew I had it in me. I think even Dreamer, on the short ride back to the farm at the time, must have been puzzled by his master's competent control. The occasional, puzzled glance over his shoulder in suspicion at my sobriety, told its own story.

"Are you ready for combat?" Vermeulen asked.

"You are the one who is going to carry the fight," I said.

He laughed. "Professor Malan said he might have found something to help our case. He will not be there to begin with but will appear in the afternoon session just before the jury deliberates."

"So, you will be handling the initial presentation and questioning—isn't it his job as lead counsel for the defense?"

"It's not necessary for him to be there in the beginning but it is for the closing argument. I believe he has something up his sleeve."

"Sounds promising," I chirped.

On arrival in Pretoria we booked into the usual hotel and spent the evening on some of the questions I might be asked if called on by the plaintiff's counsel. Vermeulen felt this might be possible so he wanted to prep me before we turned in. I lay on my bed and prayed to a God I didn't think existed. The next day would be the most important in my life.

At 11:00 am, seated at the counsel's table in front of the bench, we waited for the judge to arrive. A nervous tension gnawed at my gut as I looked around at the faces of the few people gathered to hear the outcome of the case. They comprised of law students and interested lawyers, who worked on degrees or compilation of knowledge. The eleven person jury took their seats—some looked bored and others detached.

Judge Breytenbach strolled in and the clerk shouted for everyone to rise.

After the judge seated himself we all sat down and I looked across to the plaintiff's table, at Robert King. He wore a smug look, as if in his opinion, the case would be a forgone conclusion.

The plaintiff's counsel, Mr. Sturgess, straightened his tie and stood to address the judge.

"In the case of my client verses Thomas Satherwaite Your Honor, I enter the contract signed and dated by the defendant, for the court's scrutiny. It is a legal binding document which fully declares the nature of business to be entered into. The property, Kweetsa farm is on a government lease to Mr. Thomas Satherwaite. The subjects governing the mineral rights are clearly stated as are the terms of collateral for the loan to be supplied by the CBF Company."

The judge thanked him and he sat down. Vermeulen rose from his chair.

"I am Pieter Vermeulen, counsel for the defense. I will be representing the defendant, Mr. Thomas James Satherwaite, in conjunction with Barrister Malan, Your Honor. We would like to point out the contract in question is missing certain vital dates which if entered, would have changed the entire nature of this claim by the CBF Company. We further deduce the plaintiff, Mr. King, deliberately left these vital dates out in order to have my client bankrupted through the need to supply all the initial finances to cover the excavation and export of the mineral."

The judge removed his round-rimmed spectacles and blew on the lenses. "Thank you Mr. Vermeulen I understand your concern about the dates but is it not the responsibility of the owner to make sure these things are listed?"

Vermeulen clenched the muscles in his jaw. "It certainly is a matter for the experienced, your honor, but my client is a farmer—a man of cattle-raising and agriculture. Such a person, who before he took up farming laid bricks for a vocation, is not typically vested in the fine print or details of contracts."

The plaintiff's counsel jumped in. "Your Honor, I suggest such people, like Mr. Satherwaite, should have approached a lawyer to read the contract through before signing it."

The judge considered the interruption and looked down his nose at the counselor. "If you have an objection Mr. Sturgess, I suggest you make it known as such. The court is well-versed on the protocols of objections."

Mr. Sturgess apologized and sat down but his words appeared to have been well taken by the jury. Several of them nodded their heads when he made the point.

The judge continued. "The contract is not particularly clear when it comes to the lease agreement of government property, however, and I think the plaintiff might have a problem in assuming the mineral rights pursuant to the agreement entered into by the defendant, with the Chamber of Mines."

Sturgess cleared his throat to catch the judge's attention. "Your Honor, The Chamber of mines is merely orchestrating the mineral authenticity as is the agreement between all mining companies and the government. The agreement states all minerals obtained from a Mine operation are subject to the Chamber of Mines mineral testing techniques and are bound by their prognosis."

"Thank you for the educated speech, Mr. Sturgess, but I read here in the contract: the Chamber of Mines has a direct relationship to the Government contract and these rights might not be transferable."

"There is no evidence in writing of property, or mineral rights, not being transferable your honor," said Sturgess.

The legal banter went on for two hours and at 1:00 pm the judge brought the gavel down to declare a half-hour recess. We all stood, stretched our legs and walked outside to the grass lawn beside the building.

"We're not getting anywhere, Pieter," I said.

"I know it may seem bad, Tom but be patient. Professor Malan sent word he has something up his sleeve. It will be he who carries the last part of the session."

Vermeulen held out a note in the professor's handwriting. A clerk brought it to him minutes before we left the building.

"I hope he has something substantial because the jury appears convinced I'm an uneducated moron who deserves his fate."

"Don't give up hope, Thomas," he declared.

∞∞

THIRTY-SIX

The law helps those who watch, not those who sleep. —Proverb.

By 1:30 pm the second session of court got underway. Professor Malan's absence alarmed me and I entertained the notion he would miss the most important part of the proceedings. If he didn't find the information he sought my defense might suffer a lethal blow.

The argument continued, back and forth with Vermeulen's reasons and Sturgess's rebuttals. I watched the jury and could see their often agreement with the Plaintiff's rhetoric. We drew toward the final statements and Vermeulen wiped the perspiration from his brow. The repeated glances over his shoulder at the courtroom entrance, told its own story.

The judge looked quite bored and I could see he wanted to get it over with—the verdict still required the jury's deliberation. He heard the last words of each counsellor and raised his gavel to strike the sound block, when the doors burst open to reveal Professor Malan in full flight. His cane worked overtime to support his heavy frame in a headlong dash down the aisle to our table. The briefcase flapped up and down in unison with the gyration of his gait and perspiration coursed down his face.

"I apologize for being late Your Honor but it took me longer than expected to find the information I was looking for."

The judge, annoyed at the sudden appearance, leveled his gaze at the professor. "I hope you have something of significance to add counselor because we are almost done here."

"Very significant, your honor—if the court pleases I can produce evidence for the court to reconsider the context of the main document—the contract."

"I am intrigued by you statement counselor. What is of such significance it could derail future proceedings?"

Malan composed himself. "Your Honor, I took the liberty to check a record I think my esteemed colleague, counsel for the Plaintiff may have overlooked."

Sturgess stiffened up and leaned forward at the same time.

"Carry on, Mr. Malan," said the judge.

"The original agreement between the Government and Mr. William John Satherwaite, in 1905—the lessee of the property at the time—appears to have been misfiled and therefore not brought into consideration when the CBF Company signed the contract with Mr. Thomas Satherwaite."

"And you have recovered this misfiled document?" asked the judge.

"Indeed, Your Honor. The document is the first of its kind, which explains why its implications to the contract in question are not widely known."

Sturgess and King exchanged puzzled glances.

"May I approach the bench, Your Honor?" asked Malan.

The judge beckoned and the professor stepped up to hand him a document. The judge glanced at it with raised eyebrows. He looked at Sturgess and King.

"Please tell the court what the document implies, Professor Malan."

"The document is the original agreement dictating all transactions for properties offered to individual farmers, regarding the rights of the land's use and development. It clearly states the Government does not allow secondary ownership through purchase, but by succession only. The farm can therefore never be released before a period of ninety-nine years has expired, unless there is no succession. The property was chartered to Mr. William John Satherwaite on a ninety-nine year leasehold agreement. The rights assigned with the lease of the farm cannot be passed on to anyone else other than a family member, for a period of ninety-nine years."

The judge scratched his chin and contemplated Malan's words. He removed the round-rimmed spectacles and blew on the lenses for the umpteenth time.

"So, the farm, with mineral rights, could not be held as security by another party—other than the Government."

The judge's face turned to stone as he glared in the direction of Messrs. Sturgess and King. Mr. Sturgess jumped out of his seat and objected in the strongest terms but the judge held up his hand in a gesture to stop the counsellor in mid-sentence.

"Your objection is noted Counsellor but it is a moot point. The Government document has pre-eminence over any secondary documents filed by the plaintiff or the defendant. It is unfortunate you did not do your homework, Sir. I declare a mistrial on the basis of an invalid contract. Case and jury dismissed!" The gavel slammed down on the sound block.

I couldn't believe it—the case thrown out of court due to a technicality. I looked at Vermeulen who in turn stared back at me. In my delight I hugged old Malan and laughed out aloud.

When I looked across the room at King's face, a black thunder cloud stared back at me. He shook his head, shouted at his counselor and returned a stony glare in my direction. With a wag of the finger, he stormed out of the courthouse; several people stared after him in disbelief. The jury left their chairs, dismissed as per the judge's instructions and we all filed out the doors to the street.

Later, Vermeulen, Malan and I sat in the hotel pub with a celebratory drink in hand.

"I guess you actually have reason to get smashed tonight, Thomas," said Vermeulen.

Prior to the decision in regard to my change of attitude about alcohol abuse, the lawyer's assumption would have been correct but the thought of over indulgence did not enter my head. "Not tonight, Pieter but you can go ahead if you feel like it."

He shook his head. "I'm glad you feel that way. It isn't my custom to drink more than is necessary. I guess you've had a wake-up call?"

I told Vermeulen about my decision to become a more responsible person. "The failure of my marriage and the potential loss of the farm sobered me up. The time to dispense with immature practices is before all is lost and becomes unrecoverable."

"Sounds like good wisdom to me," said Vermeulen.

I decided to take advantage of the moment and posed a question. "I'm sure you can now tell me who the mysterious benefactor is—the need for secrecy is surely over."

Vermeulen looked embarrassed. "I received a request from your benefactor to remain silent on the matter. The person implicated wants to tell you personally."

"So, I must wait—for how long?"

"When your benefactor is comfortable to divulge the information."

*

The twinkle of lights announced our arrival in the small community, nestled at the foot of the kopje.

The train, delayed at Pietersburg chugged into the Kweetsa station a bit later than usual and the veld, cloaked with soft moonlight took on the appearance of a fairytale landscape. Vermeulen and I, happy to be home again stuck our heads out of the window, to take in the cheeriness of the few buildings and single platform.

I couldn't wait to see Claire again. No thought for what she might think, I purposed to sweep her up in my arms and hold her until my shaky emotions subsided. We, the victors—Vermeulen and I, home from the war of the High Court, needed to celebrate with our friends and family. My future looked bright again but one small obstacle remained—would Claire come into partnership with me?

She needed time to consider whom she wanted to build a future with and I determined not to spoil it in anyway. Halifax might have more to offer in the way of financial support but I loved her with all my heart. His better looks and charisma may have me at a disadvantage but I possessed love and loyalty, attributes money couldn't buy.

We walked over to the hotel and I floated up the stairs on a white, puffy cloud of expectation. Pent up emotion with regard to our good news, further energized by the long train ride could no longer wait to be told. I could hear the flow of music from the piano but it didn't sound like Claire's usual style. In the saloon a host of patrons, seated at the tables and the counter, continued on with their conversations. Vermeulen stopped at the reception to reserve a room for himself while I wormed my way passed several couples on the dance floor and aimed for the bar. A man I'd never seen before, sat at the piano—pretty good at it, I thought.

I reached the counter and beckoned to old Cronje for a drink. He came over and I asked, "Have you seen Claire?"

He indicated with a nod, toward the center of the room where several couples danced to the music of the piano player. I searched each couple before my eyes located her. She danced with eyes closed and hadn't noticed me enter the room. Desmond Halifax's arms encircled her and their cheeks touched in an intimate embrace, lost in the moment to their collective thoughts.

An emotional sensation flamed through my chest cavity as the scene hit home to me. Devastation reigned and I stood with arms folded across my chest and clenched my jaw.

Old Cronje touched my arm. "They make a striking match, don't they?"

Without taking my eyes off the couple I said, "I guess she has made her choice."

The drink hit the bottom of my stomach like a hot iron. As the emotion within me subsided I decided to leave the hotel and make my way out to the farm. The stable boy brought Dreamer out from his cubicle and the two of us took off into the gloom at a fast canter.

∞∞

THIRTY-SEVEN

I am not afraid of death, I just don't want to be there when it happens. —Woody Allen.

The farmhouse felt empty. Due to the fear of wild animal attacks Letsatsi always left for the village before darkness fell. I fired up a lantern and sat down on the verandah with the dogs for company. A desolate sadness dragged on my heart whenever my mind reverted back to the scene in the hotel. I saw the woman I loved in the arms of another man—the ingredients for disaster in many a love story. It epitomized the soap-operas of the last thousand years in the saga of man meets woman and I laughed, cynical of those who thought there could ever be true romance.

The bottle of brandy in the larder called out to me and for a moment a battle raged, but I didn't give in—to do so would be the end of integrity. For once in my life the truth needed to endure. One of the Danes looked at me with soulful eyes, as if to say we're here for you, boss. I reached down to ruffle the animal's ears and triggered his tail into the usual thump routine. If people could be more like dogs—uncomplicated, always ready to serve and love their masters.

The warm air soon acted like a sleep potion and before I knew it slumber carried me away into the courtroom drama, where the judge stripped me of all my clothes and Claire who stood at the Plaintiff's table, laughed at my nakedness.

*

Old Pheko's morning yodel proclaimed, once again with repetitive monotony, the emergence of first light.

My body felt stiff from the chair's hard, wooden planks and for a moment, confusion reigned. Sunrise, more often experienced in a soft, warm bed now took on all the elements of the outdoors, before memory of the previous night, dawned on me. I yawned and considered the events at the hotel again.

While in stolid contemplation a familiar sound reached my ear—Letsatsi's soft voice offered up songs of the Kingdom in Sotho as she made her way down the path toward the farm house. I felt a sudden connection to the black maid and her people. Their lives, governed by mythical stories and accompanied by ancient tribal laws posited a simpler lifestyle—their relationships, unfettered by the complications presented by European standards.

After breakfast a hunt for venison got underway and I, with Mauser in hand, spent the day in search of buck-meat for the butchery. At about midday I stopped to rest in the shade of a Marula tree and drank from my meagre water supply. A rustle in the bushes at my rear caught my attention and I turned my head to have a look. In an instant a heavy blow caught me between the eyes, as someone jabbed a rifle-butt into my forehead. Darkness closed in and I flopped down onto my side.

Cold water brought me back to a hazy wakefulness. A strong hand grabbed my arm and hoisted me into an upright position, with my back against the tree. Several shakes of the head returned a measure of concentration as I strained to focus on a face which floated about ten inches in front of mine. Blood trickled down from my brow, into both eyes and my vision became blurry.

My attacker persisted in a close range visual investigation. A rag brushed over my forehead to clear the blood away and vision improved, enough for me to recognize a face—Robert King.

"Hello, Thomas. We meet again, but under circumstances much more to my favor."

"What are you doing here, King?" I croaked. My throat felt as dry as a desert.

"I have come to settle our little argument. You may have won in the courtroom but you are not going to win out here."

"What do you want from me?"

"I don't want anything from you, Thomas. You ruined the convenient little business I had going by destroying all those profitable contracts I used to have."

"You're a despicable fraud and a liar, King; a disgrace to the Queen's army."

King shrugged his shoulders. "I know what you think of me, Satherwaite. I did my bit for the old country and the Queen rewarded me with a medal before shoving me out to pasture. I am a soldier—not a retired, pot-bellied old has-been, who struggles to make ends meet on a piddling pension."

"What do you intend to do with me?"

"I have thought of this ever since our little day in court. Perhaps I should tie you up and leave you for the hyenas to find—or maybe I should shoot you and get it over with."

"What will killing me benefit you, King? You'll always be looking over your shoulder. There's nothing to gain from it."

He smirked, "You say I have nothing to gain? How about sweet revenge? But for your interference, my net worth would be millions of pounds. I spend years of hard work to build up my Kingdom and you brought it down with your break-and-enter caper. Those contracts were my passport to paradise."

"It was your boss who agreed to hand them over."

"Mr. so-called, Ex—is a conniving bastard who only thinks of himself."

I felt a rising tide of disgust at King's self-serving approach to life.

"You are twisted and demented, King. Your boss decided to cut you out because your life meant as little to him as the lives of all the property owners you tried to cheat, meant to you."

"Your sentimentality amuses me, Satherwaite. I am a soldier and my job in a war is to kill the opposition. You declared war on my business and you may have succeeded in robbing me of a good financial future but today, I have the final say."

"Please don't do this. You still have opportunity to make something of your life."

"I will still make something of my life, Thomas but the military taught me one thing—deal with those who oppose you. You are an expendable loose end that needs to be tied up."

"I don't believe you, King. You are nothing more than a coward."

He stepped back and picked up my Mauser. A quick look around satisfied him of our seclusion. He raised the rifle and pointed it at my head. I believed my last breath to be imminent and waited for the distinctive sound of the firearm, a sound I knew well, except this time my life hung in the balance—not an animal for the pot.

The shot came with a crack and I heard the thump of the bullet, but felt no impact. I reckoned it must have passed right through me and anticipated a delayed pain to set in— but other than the throb in my head and the wound on my forehead no palpable sensation manifested. I heard a rifle fall to the ground and with a sudden lurch King tumbled forward. I sat there, on my backside with hands on cheeks, in an attempt to fathom out why his shot missed its mark.

The next moment a woman knelt over me to cradle my face in her hands.

"Thomas—Thomas please speak to me, my love."

I felt warm tears fall on my face and still it didn't register.

I looked up, stunned. "Claire? What are you doing here?"

It all became too much for me and I passed out.

*

I awoke, on my back and felt the softness of my own mattress. I looked up into Claire's eyes, red from the tears which tumbled down her cheeks, as she stroked my forehead.

"I thought I had lost you forever, Tom." She leaned down and kissed me on the lips.

Lost for words I gazed up at her in stupefied wonder until I found my tongue. "Where did you come from? I thought I was a gonner, for sure."

"I saw that terrible man at the hotel last night and I knew he was up to no good. I tried to stop you from riding away but I was not quick enough—Dreamer had you out of earshot within minutes."

I reached up my hand to touch her cheek, her face the most beautiful sight to my eyes, looked like an angel's.

"This morning I followed him out here to the farm—you had already left on your hunt so I went to the village to get Polo and we tracked the two of you. I knew he was up to something."

"I guess he must have been stalking me most of the morning," I said.

"We lost your spoor and only found it again minutes before he tried to shoot you."

"I love you, Claire. I have been meaning to say it for ages but I didn't have the guts. When I finally plucked up the courage after the court case, I came to the hotel to see you and Halifax in each other's arms. I guess I kind of lost it."

She kissed my forehead. "I only saw you as you left through the door and old Cronje told me you appeared to be very upset. I came after you but it was too late."

"What about you and Desmond?" I asked.

"We are just friends. I know it probably didn't look like it but that's how he is—a real lady's man."

"You seemed to be enjoying it," I said.

"It's because I felt a little beholden to him but you should rest now—there is much for us to talk about. I am going to stay here until you feel better."

Although my body cried out for it I didn't want to fall sleep again for fear the present reality might be lost. I could feel her warm body next to mine, with one arm draped over my chest and her forehead against my cheek—why would I want to wake up and find a different scenario?

∞∞

THIRTY-EIGHT

Love will find a way. —*unknown.*

I felt a hand on my shoulder and a voice filtered through the foggy sub-structure of the dream—such an inconvenient time for someone to break in.

"Wake up, Thomas. You've slept for hours."

Focus and memory returned at the same time. Claire sat on the bed next to me, her sympathetic eyes locked on my forehead. I lifted my hand to my brow and felt a bandage, wrapped around my head under which a large bump protruded.

"What time is it?" I asked.

"It's four in the afternoon—you've slept through the night and most of the day."

The memory of the previous day flooded back and I groaned as the pain in my forehead intensified.

"I've called for Dr. Lombard to come in from Louis Trichardt to check you over—he will be here tomorrow at midday."

"I don't need a doctor. I'll be okay."

"You have quite a wound there, Thomas. Just lie back and relax. We'll let the doc examine you and decide what's okay."

I did as she asked and the pain ebbed. "What happened to King?"

"Fortunately for him I'm a good shot. The bullet caught the back of his left shoulder and knocked him down. Polo grabbed the Mauser to keep him under surveillance while I attended to you."

"You saved my life, Claire—He was about to kill me."

"I know, my love. But now he is in Steenkamp's custody, waiting for charges to be filed."

"You said we have much to discuss," I said.

"I know you have questions, Thomas but I wanted you to recover fully before we talked about what has happened and how we should approach the future."

"I'm recovered enough to understand one thing—." I pulled her toward me and our lips met. I held her in my embrace and she reciprocated. The softness of her body melted into mine and for the first time our intentions meshed together like two well-oiled gears. I felt a completeness.

Several moments later she released her grip and stared into my eyes. "I love you, Thomas. I'm not sure when it happened but I did come to a point when I released Willy-John and felt the need for loving again."

"It doesn't matter about the timing. As long as we both feel the same way about each other, the future is secure."

"There's something you need to know about Desmond Halifax." Claire's demeanor became serious.

"I'm all ears, sweetheart."

"Desmond proposed to me the night before last and I said no. Months ago when he talked business with me—about investing in the hotel—I made him a deal."

"What sort of deal?" I asked.

"If he put up the money to help you out of the troubles you were in I would give him a share in the businesses."

I looked at her dumbfounded. The sudden frown caused my wound some pain.

She grabbed my face with both hands. "Thomas—please listen to me. I did this for us, not for him. I desperately wanted to help you keep the farm but I didn't have the available funds."

I understood her reasons. I didn't feel anger toward her but I found it difficult to accept the fact of Halifax's involvement.

"Have you entered a contractual agreement with him?" My voice sounded a little more distant than I intended.

"No, but I gave my word. He paid all the expenses relating to your trip to England and now also the legal costs of the case against King. It's a substantial amount."

I felt a little numb. The thought of financial enslavement to Halifax by means of a partnership did not sit well with me. With him still in the picture I might still lose Claire. To find out the man I thought to be my competition saved my bacon, came as a shock.

"I can pay him back from the proceeds of the mining venture," I said.

She looked a little peeved which made me feel ashamed. I should be forever grateful for her sacrifice on my behalf. I reached out and pulled her to me. My heart felt as though it would burst.

"I am ecstatic you loved me enough to make such a sacrifice, my darling. I'm extremely grateful to you, going into bat for me the way you did and it will never be forgotten."

She looked relieved and a glimmer of a smile played on her lips. "Can we just get on with our lives in the mean time?"

"We certainly can," I answered. My hand slipped under her blouse and she melted into me again with a contented sigh. The long, sensual kiss carried with it a promise of a future filled with love and joy.

***

CONCLUSION

The hotel bustled with patrons and general expectation of growth for our community flourished. Kweetsa, now a village with a town-hall and its own post office, faced a busy and secure future. Interest from outside entrepreneurs increased and the small town boasted an elected mayor—Claire.

The businesses all showed growth and the managers stayed on for many years. Old Cronje died in 1915 at the age of seventy eight—his son stepped into his shoes to keep the legacy alive.

My decision to continue with the farm and the Mine operation set my wife free to take up the challenge—Claire and I married in the summer of 1913, after my divorce to Olivia became final. Interest in the corundum market escalated due to the war between the British and German coalitions. This advent, although not a desirable condition for many millions of people, paved the road for my future fortune and success.

The United States of America expressed interest in the mineral for the development of abrasive products for Industry and the need for advice on a contract for corundum deliveries became necessary. Young Pieter Vermeulen offered his services and years later we entered into a successful partnership together.

Polo enjoyed the position of Mine Foreman under a new appointment of a senior supervisor and Letsatsi continued to look after our homestead's domestic needs. I retired my faithful old horse, Dreamer, and put him out to pasture—he sired two beautiful young foals which brought great joy to Claire's three children before they moved on to be educated.

Before our marriage, Claire and I came to a decision with regard to my benefactor, Desmond Halifax. The three of us met at the hotel one evening to discuss the position of my loan. Although disappointed at Claire's choice of a suitor he respected her decision. He offered to accept a percentage of our business income as an investment into the community—a philanthropic gesture. We felt this to be more than generous and accepted. This money helped build the town-hall and post office plus improvements to the streets and station. We became good friends. When Desmond made the occasional visit to the community to see the benefits of his legacy, he stayed at the hotel and visited with Claire and me, on the farm.

I sat with Claire on the verandah one evening and reminisced about the long journey to our recovery and success. She reminded me of Willy-

John's words—'be careful what you wish for—.'
Would I change anything?

Maybe.

If Will had lived, our lives might have taken different paths and Claire would still be married to my brother, however, 'maybe' is a meaningless conjecture. I believe success is the product of dreams and without dreams life is reduced to a predictable mediocrity, a meaningless journey without purpose.

THE END

And so, the saga of Thomas Satherwaite ends with a dignity—through much love, sweat and tears—the sacrifice is deemed worthy of its price tag. —the Author.